If Only

If Only

Thaniel's Trials

Dale P. Rhodes, Sr.

TATE PUBLISHING
AND ENTERPRISES, LLC

If Only
Copyright © 2016 by Dale P. Rhodes, Sr. All rights reserved.

No part of this publication may be reproduced, stored in a retrieval system or transmitted in any way by any means, electronic, mechanical, photocopy, recording or otherwise without the prior permission of the author except as provided by USA copyright law.

Scripture quotations are taken from the *Holy Bible, King James Version, Cambridge*, 1769. Used by permission. All rights reserved.

This novel is a work of fiction. Names, descriptions, entities, and incidents included in the story are products of the author's imagination. Any resemblance to actual persons, events, and entities is entirely coincidental.

The opinions expressed by the author are not necessarily those of Tate Publishing, LLC.

Published by Tate Publishing & Enterprises, LLC
127 E. Trade Center Terrace | Mustang, Oklahoma 73064 USA
1.888.361.9473 | www.tatepublishing.com

Tate Publishing is committed to excellence in the publishing industry. The company reflects the philosophy established by the founders, based on Psalm 68:11,
"The Lord gave the word and great was the company of those who published it."

Book design copyright © 2016 by Tate Publishing, LLC. All rights reserved.
Cover design by Nino Carlo Suico
Interior design by Jomar Ouano
Front Cover Art Design by Antony Rozwadowski of K Art and Design

Published in the United States of America

ISBN: 978-1-68301-505-5
Library of Congress Control Number: 2016932444
1. Fiction / Christian / General
2. Fiction / Christian / Romance
16.02.11

Acknowledgments

As James 1:17 tells us, every good and perfect gift comes down to us from above. We all have gifts of one sort or another and I believe that anything positive in our lives is a gift. With all of that being said I want to first and for most thank God for the story He put into my heart. I did not plan to write anything but this story kept coming to me and would not let me be until I decided to write it down. I truly hope everyone can see themselves in these pages somewhere if not everywhere.

Mike Johnston, I want to thank you for pointing me in the right direction for so many years. I'm sorry it took me so long to get here but I hope it turns out to be worth the wait.

To my beautiful wife Phyllis, thank you for listening to my story and helping me every step of the way. You gave me story ideas, cover ideas, you typed, you proof read and listened to me all along the way.

To our sons, Dale Rhodes, Jr., Andrew Rhodes, Jeremy Bamburg and Zachary Pounsberry, thank you guys for help with the story, for typing, for giving opinions along the way.

To the rest of my family, those still with me and those who have gone on, I love you and thank you for your support.

To my niece, Angela Horne, and my friends Kelly Aylor and Ernie Leighty, thank you for proof reading and giving me your opinions.

Thank you Mike Manchas, Nikki DeRosa, Chastity Leistra, Kelly Peters and DaJuan Kenny for the encouraging words.

Thank you Doug and Donna Cherry for praying for me. It means so much to know that I can call on you to listen and pray with me when I need it.

Thank you D'Arcy Blobaum for being so nice to talk with and for answering all my questions to get me started with Tate Publishing. Thanks to the rest of the Tate Publishing team for bringing my book to life.

Thank you Antony Rozwadowski of K Art and Design for turning my stick figure drawing into a beautiful cover design.

Last but certainly not least, thank you dear reader for taking time to read my story. I truly hope that it will encourage you to move a little closer to the Lord. Just so you know, I really just wrote what God was saying to me and I hope that maybe you might find that He speaks to you as well.

From the Author

I know that there are many controversial topics in scripture that everyone simply will not agree on, and I'm sure angels are one of them. Exactly what their role is on Earth is not spelled out for us, so I hope that as you read this book, you will allow me a little creative license as I am simply trying to paint a picture of things that we all can do to share God's love with others. None of the characters in this story are based on any one real person but rather on events that I feel that we all could find ourselves in. There are, however, some things that are based on things in my life, both good and bad. It is my sincere hope that every reader can put themselves in the story somewhere or several somewheres. Let us all draw near to God for He longs to be with us. I do hope you find this book to be a good read and an encouragement.

I also thought you may like to know why I chose the names I did for the angels. I wanted names that matched the character of the angels. *Thaniel* means "Gift of God," *Haniel* means "Graciousness of God," and *Jankiel* means "Yahweh (God) is merciful."

Contents

Prologue 13

1	It Can't End Like This	17
2	No Rest for the Weary	22
3	What to Do Now?	27
4	Too Much Too Soon	31
5	Southern California, 1971	36
6	Back to Work	46
7	Not Just Yet	50
8	Fancy Meeting You Here	54
9	On His Own	60
10	Back at the Club	65
11	Come with Me, Please	70
12	It's Off to Church We Go	74
13	1950: A North Carolina Prison	79
14	Why?	84
15	At Long Last We Meet	88
16	1932: New York City	93
17	Been a While, Huh?	101

18	London 1880	107
19	Thaniel's Solace	113
20	Let's Hit the Slopes	119
21	I Never Knew	126
22	A New Day	131
23	You're Gonna What?	141
24	A New Car?	146
25	Off We Go	152
26	Oh No	156
27	In the Chapel	161
28	Please Wake Up	165

Epilogue ... 173
Companion Section ... 179
   Thaniel ... 179
      Sands ... 179
      How Long? ... 180
      It Is Time ... 181
      What Color? ... 182
   Renee ... 183
      Grip ... 183
      The Face ... 184
      I Will Sail On ... 185
      Free ... 186

Louis 187
    When, She 187
    Good-bye 188
    Without You 189
    Flame 190
    Wound 190

Tony 191
    Anticipation 191
    Wait 192
    Sunrise 193
    Whispering Cascade 193
    Interlude... 194
    Vacation 195
    Every Kiss 196

Pastor Richards 196
    Until All Your Tears Are Gone................................. 196
    In the Midst of the Thorns 197
    Here He Come (The Victory Song) 198
    Have You Considered the Saviour Today? 199
    His Ring.. 200
    'Til There Was You 202

Jason 203
- Your World 203
- Vapor 204
- My Someday 204
- Dreaming 205
- When Good-Bye Becomes Good Night 206
- Three Rings 207

Prologue
(Two Friends Texting)

Why do you insist on holding your pain in? We are your friends. Why won't you let us help you?

> How can you help me? It's my job to do on my own, and I keep failing.

You shouldn't say that. You are not failing.

> I'm not succeeding. What else would you call it?

We've been over this before. You know very well that God doesn't expect you to make decisions for people.
He only wants you and I to be an encouragement and a help, to lead people in the right ways.

> I know. I know all of that. It just seems as though I'm having no good impact on anyone's life.

The two friends continue their texting conversation for a while, both of them responding very quickly, with letters appearing almost before their fingers seem to touch the buttons. Thaniel pours his heart out to his friend, and Haniel tries his best to be an encouragement.

Jankiel just arrived.
He says to tell you hi.

> Oh wonderful. Please tell him I said hi as well and that I asked how he is feeling.

He says he is fine
and hopes you are as
well.

> Well, I am feeling a bit better. My friends are always a help.

I'm glad, but do we have to
continue texting? You know we
can just get together and sit
and talk.

> Yes, I know, but I like
> texting. It tickles me.

Haniel shakes his head and looks over at Jankiel as he shows him the phone.

> Jankiel says you are tickled
> by the fact that I don't
> particularly like texting and
> that is why you make me do it.
> He is laughing at both of us.

> Haniel, why would
> I do that to you?

Thaniel looks up from his phone and smiles. The phone chimes for another text, bringing Thaniel's eyes back down again.

> You do know that I am
> watching you grin at me,
> don't you?

> Yes, of course I know.

Thaniel looks up again and stands from the park bench that he's been sitting on. Across the beautifully landscaped field on this unusually warm December day, he sees his friends sitting on another bench looking straight at him.

Both of them are looking his way as he waves and starts to make his way over to them. He crosses the field, moving through the many people there enjoying their day, to join them.

1

It Can't End Like This

It's a bitter cold morning with gray overcast skies and a steady rain. Pastor Richards's voice is barely audible above the gusting wind, not that there are many to hear him anyway. Most of the people who did come are only here for appearance's sake. They wouldn't want to attend the reading of the will without coming to the funeral.

Shivering and holding his coat tight with his hands in his pockets, Tony leans toward his sister and says, "It figures his funeral would be on a day like today."

"Shhh," Renee responds.

"Oh, come on," he says. "You know you're thinking it too."

"That's beside the point," she scolds. "This is not the time or the place."

"Yeah, well, it's not like anyone can hear the preacher over this storm. And why should I be listening to the sermon? I mean, come on, really. Who are we fooling here, anyway? We both know Uncle Lou was not a nice guy. There's no chance he's in heaven right now," he says.

"David Anthony Edison!" Renee scolds.

"You only call me Anthony when you want to discipline me."

"Okay then, Tony," Renee says, overemphasizing his name. "Don't you talk that way."

He looks at her, half guilty, half insolent, but doesn't reply. Renee pauses, then continues, "I'm just glad Mom is not here to see this. It would have broken her heart. She was always praying for him. She must have had Pastor Richards visit him five or six times. He just wouldn't change. Just seemed to get worse."

"I know," he replies, "but he could've helped her more. He could've helped them both. He was Mom's brother." He thinks for a few seconds. "If he didn't leave us anything, this trip is gonna be such a colossal waste of time and money."

"You need to stop, Tony. Someone might hear you." Renee has to force herself not to get too loud.

Tony concedes, "All right, all right."

Off in the distance, one stands unnoticed by everyone else, but he sees all of them. He hears the preacher, the complaints, and the whispers.

A fortune, even a divided one, must certainly be worth one morning standing in the rain…or not. None of them will turn it down, though, I'm sure, he thinks to himself, disgusted by

~ If Only ~

what he's witnessing. He doesn't say a word. Anonymity must be maintained. No one would listen to him anyway, at least not in this form. He stands quietly, listening, thinking. His emotions, a raging torrent stronger than the one they are standing in, are becoming harder to hold back the longer he stands there. He loved this man, a man who never even knew he existed, and now he's gone. His mind drifts back to the countless hours spent trying to be an influence, trying to lead him to God, wanting nothing less than for him to put his life, his faith, his heart in the hands of Jesus. Now it's too late. He doesn't have to feel the bitter cold, the rain, the wind, but he wants to. He wants to experience as much of this as he can. Someone should. So he appears in the flesh. He watches. He listens. He cries. He prays.

> Is there anyone, Lord, that will cry?
> How can they stand in this rain
> with eyes that are dry?
>
> Do they not know that a soul has been lost,
> that all he's left for them
> came at too high a cost?
>
> How is it that they are so unkind?
> No thoughts are spent on the value of life.
> Only bank accounts cross these minds.
>
> They give their hearts to ash and dust,
> too blind to see
> they are slaves to their own lust.

> One by one, they go their own way.
> Making plans for tomorrow,
> when they are not guaranteed today.
>
> Oh, God, my failures consume my heart.
> I long to see a lost one found,
> to see one rescued from the dark.

"Thaniel," he hears over his shoulder, "you know this is not your fault."

He turns, his head tilted down, and almost apologetically replies, "I know, Haniel, but that doesn't make it better."

"I know. I can't make it better. I just want to make you better," he says.

Haniel steps closer and stands beside his friend. They both turn back to face the ceremony. Pastor Richards is coming to the end of his message. The look on the preacher's face says that he feels much like Thaniel. After his brief offer for counseling and a short prayer, Pastor Richards concludes the service, and the few in attendance quickly make their way to cars sitting on the edge of the cemetery driveway.

"I'm supposed to guard them and help them find their way to God," Thaniel says, sighing in frustration.

"You do, Thaniel. You're very good at it too," Haniel says, trying to say something to help but knowing it won't.

Thaniel didn't reply. He just stood there watching.

Haniel suddenly spoke energetically, "You know I'm your best friend, and I wouldn't lie to you."

Thaniel looked over at him, knowing his friend was desperately trying to ease his pain and, with a half smile, said, "You wouldn't lie to me because you're my best friend or because we're angels and don't lie?"

Embarrassed, Haniel responds, "Both." He shrugs his shoulders and grins. "At least I got a little smile out of you."

"That you did," Thaniel says. "Come on, let's go."

2

No Rest for the Weary

The storm passed as evening comes, and a stillness rests over the town. The funeral is over, and Renee and Anthony have gone back to the hotel. They drove in together and shared the cost of a room. Anthony is in the shower. He was a gentleman and let Renee get hers first. She is sitting on her bed flipping through channels on TV, but she is in a faraway place inside. Nothing catches her interest, but by habit alone, she stops on all her favorite channels. Her mind drifts back to the many sermons from Pastor Richards she had heard as a child, and even though the wind was too strong to make out what he was saying today, it was almost as if she knew what he was going to say before it came out. Neither Renee nor Anthony wanted to go to church growing up. There were too many old people and not enough kids, and it all just seemed so boring. Their parents, Jim and Mary Ann, became Christians somewhere during the twins' middle schools years, and, of course, they were forced to come along to every horrible service. At least it seemed horrible to them, every week singing the same old hymns and shaking hands. They just hated it all. Everyone seemed so stiff and dull. So when graduation came for the twins, they made plans to get out of there.

Anthony comes out of the bathroom, sweatpants on and a towel hanging over his head as he brushes his teeth.

"Really? The House of Representatives channel?" Anthony blurts out in disbelief.

Renee just stares at the screen, remote in hand. The only sign of life is the faint movement from her breathing.

"Hello, hello, earth to Renee," Anthony says, snapping the fingers of his free hand, toothpaste dripping from his mouth.

She's in another world, so he walks over and reaches for the remote. She finally notices him.

"You okay?" he asks, this time concerned that maybe something happened while he was in the shower.

"What? Yeah , I'm sorry I was just thinking," Renee says quietly, shaking her head as she snaps out of her trance.

"I'm almost afraid to ask," he curtly replies.

"Oh…nothing…everything. I don't know. I was just thinking about the sermon at the graveside," she says with a weary look on her face. "It's just been so long since we've been to church. I just don't think about those things much anymore. You know the funeral and Uncle Lou and everything." She sat there looking into her hands. "I mean, he lived his whole life, and only a handful of people came to say good-bye, and we were the only family. That just seems so messed up."

"Look, I know this kinda thing can upset you, but you aren't like Uncle Lou. Tons of people will be at your funeral," he says, trying his best to be comforting but realizing how awful it sounded once he let it out. "I don't mean…you know what I mean."

"Tons, huh? Yeah, I know what you mean," she says, shaking her head and trying to smile. "I just love it when you put your foot in your mouth, Mr. Confident."

"Yeah, I'm getting tired of tasting leather and rubber, though," he quipped.

"I just think it so sad to live your life alone like that, and then what if…what if he didn't go to heaven?" she says, her eyes welling up.

Anthony sighs, wishing he could escape this conversation altogether. He didn't want to dismiss it, though, because that would just upset Renee, and he's always tried to take care of his twin sister. He went back to the bathroom to rinse his mouth out. Taking a deep breath, he walked back out, scrubbing his hair dry some more with the towel and then tossing it back into the bathroom. Walking over timidly, he sits down beside Renee. Speaking with a softer tone this time, he says, "I don't know, sis. I don't know about any of this. I try real hard not to think about it. It's just too depressing. I'd rather just live my life and have a good time."

Still very much disturbed by everything, she replies, "But don't you ever wonder about it all? I mean, God and death and heaven and hell. I mean, we can't avoid it forever, can we?"

Ready to give up, Anthony says, "I guess not. I just think it seems so hard. I mean who's right? Who's wrong? I remember all the preaching from when we were younger, but I mean, the people we knew didn't seem to be the same when we saw them out on the street. Aren't Christians supposed to be so happy? It just doesn't seem that way when you see them away from church. I don't understand it."

"Mom and Dad were, don't you think? I mean, not every minute of the day, but you know, in general," she says. "Maybe some people don't handle things in life well, I don't know. I'm just afraid of ending up like Uncle Lou," Renee says, her eyes showing the fatigue and stress of the day.

"I guess, and no, I don't want to end up like that either, but we have time to figure things out, don't we? I mean, we don't have to have all the answers tonight, do we?"

Anthony really doesn't want to be thinking of all the things Renee had made him think about and is desperately trying to end the conversation before they ended up still talking about it when the morning comes.

"I think I'm gonna hit the hay, sis, okay?" he says, lying back on his bed and cutting off the nightstand light.

"Yeah, I'm tired too. Good night."

Even though she turned over to get comfortable, she couldn't stop thinking, and it took her a couple of hours before she finally was able to drift off to sleep.

3

What to Do Now?

Morning finds Thaniel alone again and walking through town a little before daybreak. He does this often. It helps him to feel more connected to everything. Taking in all that he can makes him feel like he belongs there. Sights, smells, sounds, temperature, and the weather—it is all different from a human perspective, and he wants to be as close to the world as he can be. Yes, there are rules about how he is to appear and how he is to carry himself, and, yes, he does follow them, but there is nothing quite like firsthand knowledge. Thaniel knows he cannot be a part of everything that humans do, but he is drawn to the vulnerability of fallen man and wants to experience as much of this life as he can. In the end, he doesn't want to be a part of man's world. He wants man to be a part of his.

So many people, he thinks to himself, *getting up and preparing for the day*.

As he walks, he watches lights come on here and there up and down the street.

"Where are they all going? What are they thinking as they go through their morning rituals? Are they even thinking at all? Are they ready for what this world has in store for them today?" he asks himself, though he knows that most of them are not really ready.

Most of them are completely oblivious to the dangers all around them, and, to a certain extent, it's better that way. They would go crazy if they were aware of everything that makes up their world, both physical and spiritual. The thing that concerns him is that most of them are not seeking God today. They just get up and go. Not thinking of what might happen, like every day is just like the next. They think they are in control of things, when that couldn't be further from the truth.

As the sun finally breaks through the darkness, Thaniel blends back into the background and walks unnoticeable. Continuing this morning trek, he thinks back to the years of mornings that passed while he was watching over Louis Hamilton. Louis was always up before the sun, so focused, so disciplined. His business instincts were fierce, almost primal. No detail was ever overlooked. He was so carefully driven, methodical in his preparations for every move he made. He was determined to be the best, to get exactly what he wanted, and he usually did.

"No, no, no, I don't care what you have to do. Just make it happen. I need those parts on a truck today so I can fill my orders on time," Louis barked into his Bluetooth earpiece, which was around his ear more hours of the day than it was not, even now as he was getting his morning shave.

"Look, I do understand no one likes working overtime, but the other end of the scale is no orders at all. Would your team rather be laid off? Hamilton windows and doors are the industry standard for one reason and one reason only—my customers get *what* they want *when* they want it, period. Now make it happen, or I'll start looking for another supplier. You don't want to lose my contract," he says as he ends the call.

Charles, the butler, cleans his face and neck with a hot towel and pulls away the one that was covering his shoulders and chest.

Louis steps up out of the chair and with a silent nod gives recognition that the job is done. Then he puts on his jacket and straightens his tie (not that it ever needs straightening). Charles, or rather Grayson, as Mr. Hamilton calls him, when he does bother to speak, hands him his briefcase and walks him to the front door, opening it to reveal the car already waiting outside.

"Good day, Mr. Hamilton," speaks Charles. Louis returned his greeting with the customary nod.

Louis steps out to the car, where he is greeted by his driver, who is holding the door for him. Another nod and he gets in the car and is on his way to the office.

"His whole morning spent without ever speaking a word to those whom he had entrusted to help him prepare for each day," Thaniel said, though no one was there to hear it. "Such a shame. He wasn't always like that. He used to be so warm and loving."

Today's walk is uncharacteristically long. Emptiness is setting in, and Thaniel doesn't know what to do with himself.

Haniel and Jankiel, concerned for their friend, silently follow him throughout the remainder of his journey. Afraid to come too close, they simply let him mull over his thoughts until it appears he has worked through the frustration, and he makes his way back to a better frame of mind.

4

Too Much Too Soon

"No, I'm sorry. I can't do this tonight. It's too soon," she says as she pushes him away.

"Just relax, everything is okay," he replies, sounding more like a used car salesman than a date.

"No, it's not okay," she snaps. "You're pushing too much."

Anthony sits up, sighing a very weighted sigh, and then leans against the backrest of the sofa, running both hands through his thick hair. "Hey, look, you're the one that invited me over for a cozy night at your place. What is it you want?"

Tina sits straight up and takes a breath. "I invited you over for a dinner and a movie. You're just not satisfied with that."

"You're sending out too many mixed signals," he retorts.

"I had hoped you might be different than so many other guys I've gone out with." She gets up and walks over to the sink and throws some water up on her face, then dries it with a towel. He gets up and follows her over.

"You know, I had heard of you from other girls, but I figured they were exaggerating," she says, frustrated.

"Oh, you've heard of me, huh?" he says sarcastically.

"Yeah, as a matter of fact, I have. He's a looker and a smooth talker, but he's only out for one thing. Oh, and let's not expect him to hang around too long either," she blurts out.

"So that's what they say? I'm a sweet-talkin' looker? Doesn't sound so bad to me," he says smugly, leaning against the counter and crossing his feet.

"It's not a compliment, Tony. You know, I really didn't feel like a date tonight because I had a hard day at work and it's pouring down outside. I was just hoping we could just sit and have a good evening together."

Anthony seems agitated now, maybe more than he should.

"So let's recap here," he says belligerently. "You turn me down after sending out clear signals."

"Anthony, it's not like that."

"Then you insult me."

Tina sighs and shakes her head while rolling her eyes.

"Then you have me come out in the rain so you can stay dry."

"Okay, you know what, I think we need to just stop right here," she says, holding her hand up toward him.

"Yeah, we do. I'm outta here."

"Fine."

Anthony walks out, and Tina slams the door behind him, just barely missing his foot. He storms down to his car, thinking to himself, *There's always something with these girls. Everything has to be their way. I'm sick of it.*

Deciding he wants a drink, Anthony drives to the club. His thoughts quickly turn back to women as he walks toward the bar, scanning the crowd for prospects.

"Looking for someone?" he hears over his shoulder and turns to see who the words came from. His eyes perk up as they catch the sight of the owner of that beautiful voice that questioned him.

"Just you, babe, just you."

The young woman looks at him as if they already know each other. "You did not really just feed me that cheesy line, did you?" she says, her eyebrows raised and her lips pursed.

"Well…," Anthony says as he leans in a little closer. "That depends on whether or not it worked."

With a little laugh, she touches his forearm. "I'm ashamed to say, yeah, a little bit."

"Well, that's a start now, isn't it?" Anthony holds out his right hand. "Hi, I'm Anthony."

"So you really don't recognize me, huh? That is always a wonderful feeling."

Anthony, now beginning to get a little red in the face, with a few drops of sweat forming on his forehead, stutters as he speaks. "Uh, of course I recognize you. It's just been a while. You're Kaaa—" he says, not able to finish his thought because she decides to end his misery and his charade.

"Adrianna. It's Adrianna," she says, pulling her hand away from his. "We went out a couple of years ago. You said you were going out of town for business and would call me when you got back. None of this ringing any bells?"

Now totally embarrassed, he figures he must own up to his behavior if he has any chance of salvaging the evening. "Yeah, I remember now. Sorry about that."

"So you been gone all this time or what?" she says with a punishing smile, knowing she has him dead to rights.

"No. You got me," he says, looking at the floor. "Don't suppose you could see it in your heart to forgive me?" he asks, not at all expecting her to.

"Well, I really shouldn't, but I suppose we all need a little forgiveness from time to time," she replies as he sighs in relief. "So, Mr. Anthony, are you here to look or to dance?" Adrianna says, as if sending out a challenge.

Anthony holds out his hand as he smiles even wider. "Oh, I'm always ready to dance."

Taking his hand, she pulls him out to the floor, and they disappear among the sea of bouncing and swaying bodies.

After a couple hours of dancing and talking, Adrianna walks Anthony back to the bar.

"Well, Mr. Anthony," she says with a good-bye tone to her voice. "I think this is gonna do it for me tonight, so I guess I'll leave you here where I found you."

Chuckling, he responds. "Okay, I guess that's only right. So what do ya think? Like to do this again sometime?"

Holding her chin and tilting her head with a puzzled look on her face, she says, "Hmm, let's see. What to do? Oh, all right, I suppose so." Getting a scrap of paper from the bar tender, she jots down a few words and hands it to Anthony. Leaning in, she kisses him on the cheek and then pulls away. "Bye," she says and then turns and leaves him alone at the bar once more.

Holding the note, he watches her walk away.

5

Southern California, 1971

The sun is about to set on a Southern California beach.

The breeze is soft and warm, the sky a beautiful shade of orange and red on the horizon. Stars speckle the opposite side of the sky, high above small campfires dotting the beach as people enjoy another summer Friday night. Thaniel sits on a beach towel watching a special event unfold.

Off in the distance, there is a young man down on one knee holding the hands of a young woman. She nods her head, with tears streaming down her face. He jumps to his feet, picking her up, and they hug and spin around before falling to the sand as the waves reach up to them. They lay on their backs, looking up at the stars with their heads touching. She raises her left hand into the air.

"Virginia Hamilton….Mrs. Louis Hamilton," she says, smiling and turning to look at him.

"I like it," he adds.

"Ooohh!" she gasps. "Does that mean—?"

"Yes, it does." They are facing each other now. "I got a job! You know how many resumes I sent out since graduation, right? Sooo I start Monday. At the bottom for now, but one day, I will own my own company."

"I believe that, but I don't want you to spend all your time at work. I want you home with me," she says, smiling.

"That sounds good too, doesn't it?"

"Yes, it does, sweetheart. Yes, it does." She leans in and kisses him.

Another Friday afternoon, several months later, Mrs. Virginia Hamilton stands in the kitchen of the little house that she and her new husband have made a home. Smiling and humming while she works, her heart is joyful at the thought of the special evening she is planning for her husband. He should be home at five thirty, so she has timed everything accordingly. There is a large blanket and a beach umbrella by the door. Under her clothes, Virginia is wearing her swimsuit. Louis's swim trunks are laid out on their bed, along with his sandals and a short-sleeved shirt. Virginia is packing a picnic supper, and in the bottom of the basket, under the paper plates, she lays an envelope. It is Louis's birthday, and she is determined to make it a special night. There is a gallon of sweet tea in the refrigerator and a cooler full of ice sitting by it. She has made potato salad and baked beans and a peach cobbler for dessert. Chicken is in the frying pan on the stove. The house is immaculate.

Virginia and Louis believe that everything has a place and that everything should be in its place.

Their small Craftsmen-style house would not be looked at as a successful businessman's home by most, but she is thrilled with it. Like most couples, she cleans and maintains the inside, and the perfectly manicured lawn is Louis's domain.

In between the sound of grease bubbling in the pan, she hears a car pull into the driveway. Looking at her watch brings a smile as she confirms that Louis is right on time. Not wanting to wait any longer, she goes to the door and opens it to wait for him.

"Hi, sweetheart," he says as he leans in to kiss her. "How was your day?"

"It was good, dear. How was yours?" she replies, taking his briefcase from him.

"Pretty good, but it is even better now." He kisses her again. "What's all this?" he asks as he looks over her shoulder to see the picnic basket.

Smiling as she pulls away and, turning toward the kitchen table, she says, "A birthday dinner for my birthday boy."

He leans toward the basket. "I don't see a birthday cake," he says jokingly.

"Well, maybe you're an imposter then because my birthday boy would be looking for a birthday peach cobbler," she quickly retorts.

"No, no, I'm the right guy, just checking. Thank you, sweetheart." He kisses her again.

~ If Only ~

"You're welcome. Now you go change. I laid out your beach clothes. Tonight is a special night, so we need a special location," she says. "Oh, and I forgot the towels. Can you get them?"

"Sure, I won't be long."

Virginia quickly puts together the rest of the dinner and gets it ready to go.

A perfect, warm, breezy evening greets them as they carry their picnic goodies to the beach.

"All right, you go get your feet wet while I set up the blanket and dinner," Virginia says.

"Sweetheart, I can help you."

"It's your birthday. I don't want you working more than you already have to."

"But—"

"Shoo, go! Get your feet wet."

Louis smiles and shakes his head, reluctantly slipping his feet out of his sandals and heading to the warm white foam that is racing up the beach toward him. He stands in the waves looking out on the horizon, thinking of just how perfect an evening she has made for him. After a couple of minutes, he feels a soft warm hand snuggle up against his, and he holds tight to it and looks over to see his wife. "You are so beautiful," he says. "In fact, I've never seen you more beautiful than you are right now."

Virginia kisses him and then lays her head on his shoulder and puts one hand on his stomach and the other around his waist.

"I love you, dear," she says.

"I love you too."

After dinner, she holds up the peach cobbler and his birthday card. "Dessert and card now or after a swim?" she says.

"How about we walk off the dinner and then have a swim?" he replies, holding out his hand. "Then we'll have the pie and the card."

"All right, whatever my birthday boy wants," she says, slipping out of her flip-flops and stands, taking his hand.

Together they go off down the beach. Virginia stops and leans to the ground.

"What's the matter, dear?" Louis says, leaning down to see if perhaps she has stepped on something.

Playfully she splashes him with ocean water and runs off down the beach.

"Oh, it's gonna be like that tonight, huh?" he says and takes off after her. He catches her more quickly than he should, which means she has slowed up to let him since she is very athletic and usually beats him in every sport they play.

"Come here you," he says, grabbing her waist and turning her while he lifts her off the beach into the warm

~ If Only ~

California breeze. "What has gotten in to you tonight?" he says, smiling.

"Just enjoying the evening with my handsome man at the beach." She smiles back at him as if she is about to burst. "What could be any better than that?"

Thaniel, again sitting on a beach towel, watches another special moment between Louis and Virginia Hamilton.

They are so good for each other, he thinks to himself. *I have succeeded in getting them together. Now it's time to start sewing some Gospel seeds.*

He continues watching them as their footprints follow them across the beach.

After they had a nice swim, Virginia asks, "Are you ready for dessert?" She moves toward the beach.

"Oh no, it's my turn to get things ready. You've worked enough today. Enjoy a few more minutes," Louis insists.

"All right, dear. Just a little more."

Thaniel watches Louis setting up the dessert, cutting the pie, pouring the tea, and setting out the birthday card envelope.

Louis stops to look at the envelope and sees the words "My handsome man" on the front. He is tempted to pull it out and read it but does not because Virginia is not there. Setting it down on the blanket, he looks everything over and checks the basket for anything he may have missed. He abruptly stops and raises his head, thinking he hears something, something faint, but he can't quite make it out above the sounds of sand and surf.

"What is that?" he says after hearing the noise again. He turns to see where the sound is coming from. "There it is again. It's a scream." Back and forth, he looks but cannot make out the sound.

"Virginia!" His mind now figures it out. Frantic, he looks around to find her.

Thaniel is now jumping up from his blanket and running into the water, catching Louis's eyes. Before Thaniel can reach her, Virginia goes down under the surface by the power of a rip current. Louis starts running frantically to catch up. When Thaniel realizes what it is, he turns to yell to Louis, "It's a rip current! Stop! Wait there!"

Louis does not stop and reaches Thaniel just as he emerges from the Pacific with Virginia in his arms. The life guard is right behind him, and they carry her back to the beach and lay her down. Another lifeguard now arrives, and the two quickly begin CPR. Thaniel, frustrated and unable to do anything more because of all the onlookers, waits with everyone else.

"Please be okay, sweetheart. Please save her," Louis cries out now, fully engulfed in the horror of the moment.

~ If Only ~

Compression after compression, breath after breath, nothing.

"She's not responding," Thaniel says.

Louis now drops to his knees and takes Virginia's hand. "Please, sweetheart, stay with me. Please don't leave. Please, God, don't take her," he cries as he looks to up to heaven.

Compression after compression, breath after breath, nothing.

"No, no, no, nooo! Don't take her! Don't take her!" Screaming and crying, Louis can't even see through the tears now. As he stops to catch his breath, he hears sirens approaching. An ambulance pulls as close as they can, and EMTs jump out, pulling a gurney across the sand. As quickly as possible, in between the compressions, she is strapped onto the gurney. Still holding her hand, Louis follows with her to the ambulance.

"Do you have a car, sir?" one of the EMTs asks.

"I'm riding with her."

"Of course, sir, but can someone come pick you up?"

Louis quickly scans the crowd and points to Thaniel.

"Can you bring my car?" He tosses the keys. "It's the blue Ford."

"Uh…all right. You go. I'll find you," he replies.

"Louis and Virginia Hamilton," he says.

The doors shut, and the ambulance speeds away.

"If I can fly, I can drive this thing," Thaniel says as he looks at the car.

Arriving at the hospital, Thaniel finds Louis in the chapel, alone. When he sits down beside him, Louis just looks at him. Thaniel knew what the look meant.

"I'm sorry," Thaniel says.

Louis sits motionless, his face as pale as a ghost, his mind, his heart, and his life shattered in a moment of time.

"If there is anything I can do?" Thaniel tries to say but is cut off.

"If you can bring her back," Louis whispers.

Thaniel just breathes.

"If you can convince God not to keep her, to give her back to me," he speaks with just enough volume to be heard, his strength gone.

"I don't know. I don't understand," Thaniel offers.

Louis just turns and, with a stonewalled gaze, pierces Thaniel straight in the heart.

Louis sits silently, frozen in thought.

"We must trust the Lord knows best even when we do not," Thaniel forces out, not knowing what else to say.

"He has taken everything from me and you expect me to trust Him?" Louis snaps.

Thaniel, not knowing what to say, asks, "Can I take you home?"

"Home to what? I don't know?"

"We can just sit in the car awhile if you like," Thaniel squeaks out.

~ If Only ~

"I do appreciate you coming…" Realizing he doesn't know his name, he just looks at him, confused.

"Thaniel," he says. "My name is Thaniel."

Louis sits in the passenger side, his feet beside the picnic basket.

"I hope I didn't mess everything up," Thaniel says, pointing to the basket.

Louis opens it to find the birthday card. He slowly pulls it from the basket and then from the envelope. Tears running down his face as he opens the card, he reads, "Happy birthday, my darling. I love you, but you will have to wait nine months for your present. I'm pregnant."

Sobbing now, he cries out, "Why! Why, why did I leave her alone! Why?" Louis heaves and is barely coherent.

"You can't blame yourself. It's not your fault," Thaniel says.

"I don't. I blame Him." Louis looks at Thaniel while pointing to the sky. "I blame God."

"You must trust—" Thaniel starts but is quickly interrupted.

Louis hands the card to Thaniel. "Not today. Maybe not ever."

6

Back to Work

Renee is sitting at her desk at work, trying to savor just a few moments of peace and finishing her lunch. Her hand is raising to take another drink of hot chocolate from her mug when the boss, Mr. Caldwell, comes in.

"Hi, Renee," he says and stops at her desk. "How are you doing today? I hope it hasn't been a tough one. I have been thinking about you and your family."

In that moment, a moment which she would normally just say, "I'm fine and thank you," she could no longer hold back the emotions of the last several days.

"Well, Mr. Caldwell, since you asked," she says, "while I do very much appreciate you thinking of me and my family, I'm not really doing well at all today."

Mr. Caldwell stands up straighter, a bit surprised, and says, "Is there anything I can do to help?"

"I don't know what you could do. I guess nothing. Why would you even think that there is something you could do? Because you're a big strong man and I'm a defenseless woman?" Renee's agitation grew with every word. "Or is it because you are the rich and powerful big boss man and I should be grateful you are here?"

Mr. Caldwell, in shock, replies, "Well…no…I—"

"No, of course not, you didn't mean any of that, did you? No, you were just trying to help," Renee says sarcastically.

The sound of the emotional torrent now reaching down the hall way brings a few heads out to peer around the open doorways.

"Well, maybe there is something you can do. Although you're a bit late at this time, but maybe it would be nice if someone else could do just a bit of the work while I'm out so I'm not overwhelmed when I come back from a couple of days off." She is almost shouting now.

Mr. Caldwell, not sure what to say at this point, stands silent and still. All at once, Renee bursts into tears. Now Mr. Caldwell is kicking himself inside for not having walked away. Desperately searching for the right words to say, he timidly speaks, "Renee, why don't we go to my office?"

"It's just been so hard over the last few days," she says, still crying.

"Well, I'm sorry."

"I know I wasn't close to Uncle Louis, but I didn't want him to die."

"Oh…of course."

"And that's another thing. He lived and died alone. Maybe I should have tried harder to connect with him," she says, tears dripping onto the legal papers on her desk.

Mr. Caldwell, noticing this, tries to move them from the line of fire. As he moves the documents, Renee holds on to his hands. His eyebrows now raised, he looks down the hallway to the heads still sticking out past their doorways. He shrugs as if to say, "I have no idea what's next."

"And of course, thinking of my uncle makes me think of my parents. I miss them so much." She is now in a full-blown bawling fit. "Why did they have to be in a stupid car crash? Why did they have to leave us? They were so good and kind. Always going to church. Always trying to help others."

"Yes, well, I'm sure."

"I know, I know. They are in a better place now. But what about Uncle Lou? Where is he? I can't stand the thought."

Her nose, now running, quickly catches Mr. Caldwell's attention, and he pulls his hand free. Reaching for the handkerchief in his lapel pocket, he grabs it and instantaneously offers it to Renee, who takes it and begins to blow her nose. The sound, reminding him of a foghorn, makes him wish he had a boat to catch.

"Thank you," she says, continuously sobbing. "Poor Uncle Lou."

"That's quite a—" he tries again but is again cut off.

"And what does that mean for me? I mean, I haven't been to church in a long time. What if I die?" she cries out again.

"Oh, well, I'm sure you would—"

"But how do you know that? How can I know? What do you think? What should I do? What about you? What are you gonna do?"

Mr. Caldwell, now frozen in place, is afraid to go but afraid to stay. Renee finally finishes blowing her nose and, wiping it, offers the handkerchief back to Mr. Caldwell with one last sob. "Thank you."

"Oh no, my dear…you…you keep it." He sighs.

She nods, which he takes as permission to leave, and begins to turn toward the hallway.

"You know," she says, stopping him in his tracks. "I know you mean well, but you'd be a whole lot more help if you would talk some."

He raises his head slightly but is afraid to look at her again and slowly walks toward his office.

"Renee? Renee! Are you all right?" Mr. Caldwell asks.

Renee shakes her head and blinks a couple of times, waking from her daydream. "Yeah. Oh yes, I'm just fine. Thank you, Mr. Caldwell."

7

Not Just Yet

"Yeah, hang on. I got it," Adrianna says as she reaches in the drawer and finds a lighter. "Okay, here it is."

Flick, flick.

The lighter finally bursts out flame, and Adrianna lights eight candles on her niece's birthday cake.

"Does she seem to be enjoying her party?" Adrianna's sister asks as she scoops ice cream onto ten plates and places them on a serving tray.

"Are you kidding me? Look at her. She's having a blast. Nine good friends and she is the center of attention. Yes, she is having a good time. Are you ready?"

"Yep let's go."

Buzz, buzz, buzz.

"I'm sorry, wait just a second. It's my phone." Adrianna pulls her cell phone from her pocket and reads the text message appearing.

> Can I see you tonight?

~ If Only ~

"Everything all right?" Emily asks.

"Yeah. It's the guy I told you about. He wants to see me tonight," Adrianna replies.

"Sweetie, it's okay if you want to go."

"No, it's not. I like him, but he has to learn I love my family and I'm not gonna just drop everything in my life for him," she says as she puts her phone back in her pocket and picks up the cake. "I'll text him in a minute. Let's do the cake."

"Okay. Why don't you tell him to come over here?"

"I did. He wants to go out."

"I just can't get over the change in you lately."

Adrianna smiles.

"I mean, not so long ago, you would have rather gone out dancing instead of a birthday party for kids."

They walk through the kitchen carrying cake and ice cream and set them around the dining room table.

"I guess I see things differently now. It's like God has opened my eyes, and I see what's important now. I still love to dance, but I didn't want to miss this."

Emily's husband sees them setting the table and calls all the girls to come. "All right, girls. Looks like it's time to have the birthday girl blow out the candles."

The girls all settle in around the table, and Adrianna's niece makes a wish and blows out the candles as everyone cheers and sings.

"Happy birthday to you, happy birthday to you, happy birthday, dear Mia, happy birthday to you."

Buzz, buzz, buzz.

Adrianna's phone vibrates again. She pulls it out of her pocket and motions to her sister that she is going back to the kitchen.

> What do you say? Are we on for tonight?

I'm at my niece's birthday party. Why don't you come over here? My sister would love to meet you.

> Maybe another time.

I'm really sorry, but this is important to my niece. I just couldn't miss it.

> It's ok. Don't worry about it.

Ok, thank you. Call me later?

> Yeah sure.

Adrianna puts her phone away again and walks back into the party.

"Is he coming?" Emily asks.

"No. He said another time," Adrianna replies. "He's gonna call me later."

Her sister hands her a plate with cake and ice cream. "Here you go, sis. I can't be the only one here with calories to burn tomorrow."

"Gee thanks. You make it sound so appealing."

8

Fancy Meeting You Here

It's Saturday afternoon, and Renee is leaving the café near her apartment. After having slept late, she had brunch with a couple of her friends from work. Her friends, both of whom are married, have planned a double date for tonight, which makes Renee a fifth wheel. So having no plans herself for the evening, she decides to get her groceries for the week, something she normally does on Sunday. Then she plans to rent a movie and pig out on popcorn and ice cream and most likely fall asleep on the couch. As she walks down the street, the afternoon breeze blows by a small flyer advertising a church event. Renee stops to pick it up, reading, "Dave and Pearl Richards."

Hmmm, she thinks. *That's Pastor Richards. I wonder what this is about.* She continues to walk and read until she reaches her apartment. After changing into jeans and a T-shirt and going to the bathroom, she is ready to leave. Picking up the flyer again, she notices the address for the church is different than what she remembers it to be. On her way out the door, she grabs her purse and brings the flyer along, deciding to drive by and see this new location.

As Renee looks at the new, bigger building, she has a greater wonder of what the event was that the flyer was advertising. Her thoughts run back to her parents, and she tries to remember if they had mentioned having a new church building. She and Anthony never liked talking with their parents about church and God after they left home. They would usually either tune them out or change the subject, so she couldn't think of a time when a new building was mentioned. Putting the flyer back in her purse, she pulls out of the church parking lot and heads for the grocery store. Being on this side of town she decides to try the store near the church.

Thoroughly lost and confused in the new environment, Renee starts to think she has made a huge mistake stopping at this store. Focused on finding the oatmeal, she doesn't hear her name called.

"Renee, Renee!"

Finally the sound breaks through her concentration, and she looks up to see Pastor and Mrs. Richards.

"Hi, dear, how are you?" Mrs. Richards asks, giving her customary hug.

"Oh, hi. I'm okay," she replies, surprised to have run into them. "I'm sorry I didn't see you. I'm in my own little world here."

"That's okay. I think I stay in a different world most of the time. Don't I, dear?" the pastor says and chuckles a little.

"I'm so glad we ran into you, Renee," Mrs. Richards says. "I've been thinking of you lately."

Pastor Richards takes the opportunity, while his wife is talking, to slip some cookies into the basket, hoping she won't notice until they are home, but, of course, she does and cuts him a look.

"Sweetheart, man can't live on sweets alone," she says and looks at Renee and smiles. He smiles too and puts in another box while holding his finger up in front of his lips an making the "shhh" motion to Renee, who tries not to laugh at him.

"So, yeah, it's funny that I ran into you two today," Renee says. She searches through her purse and brings out the flyer. "I found this fly—"

"Ooh, ooh, I've got it!" the pastor breaks in. He then looks at Renee and says, "I'm so sorry to interrupt. I just had an idea." Turning to his wife, he says, "Sweetheart, paper, I need a piece of paper."

"Your pocket, dear. Check your pocket," she replies.

He frantically starts checking his jacket pockets, then his inside pockets.

"Dear," his wife says as she reaches into his lapel pocket and pulls out a small notepad and pen and holds it up in front of him.

He smiles and takes it from her. Mrs. Richards, without skipping a beat, turns back to Renee as she shakes her head and rolls her eyes toward her husband. "Now, dear, what were you saying?"

Renee smiles. "Just a little while ago, I found this flyer on the street just down from my apartment. I noticed Pastor Richards's picture on it, so it's funny that I ran into you guys today."

Mrs. Richards looks at the flyer. "Oh yes, this is for our service tomorrow. We mailed out quite a few and handed out some as well." She looks over at her husband and then back at Renee. "He is starting a new series on the end times tomorrow. A ten-week study."

"Oh, okay. Sounds intense," Renee says.

"I'm sure it will be. End-time studies usually raise a few eyebrows," Mrs. Richards comments.

"Okay, how does this sound?" Pastor Richards says. "You've changed me from the man I used to be, so help me live, Lord, like I'm free."

"That sounds nice. What is it?" Renee asks.

"An idea for a song. Well, an idea for a line in a song. It just came to me," he replies and goes back to writing in his notepad.

"Okay. Let me get this straight. I scold you for eating too many sweets, and you come up with a line for a song about living like you're free?" Mrs. Richards snaps. "Just what are you trying to be free from?"

For just a second, he has the deer-in-the-headlights look on his face. Then he asks her, "How are you so quick at getting me with those things?"

She shrugs her shoulders. "It's simple, sweetheart. You set yourself up all the time. I can't turn away from all of them," she says with a grin.

He looks at Renee and says, "Do you see how she treats me?"

"Sounds rough." Renee giggles.

"He is so blessed," Mrs. Richards says.

"Yes, I am, dear," he says and then winks at Renee and smiles. "You see, that's the secret to my being blessed. I just agree with everything she says."

"Okay, okay. Let's get back to reality now," Pearl says. "So what do you think, sweetie? Can you come? We would love for you and Anthony to make it out."

"Yeah, seriously, Renee. I know you and Anthony were not really happy with church growing up, but I think you'll find it to be different now," David says.

"Well…I don't know," Renee answers as she begins nervously fiddling with her hair. "I mean, I'll have to talk to him, but I guess I can make it.

"Look, please don't just say no. Think it over. Sleep on it. I know we were a small church back then, mostly older people. Today it's different. We have a really good mix of age, gender, and race. Very energetic. I will leave it at that, but I do want you to know that we are always here for you two, okay?" he says.

"It was really nice seeing you again, dear. Please tell Anthony we said hi," Mrs. Richards says.

"Okay, I will. Good to see you both too," Renee answers, watching them walk away down the aisle and turn the corner out of her sight. "Oh man, I just know he is not going to like this."

9

On His Own

Stood up for a birthday party. That's gotta be an all-time low for me, Anthony thinks to himself as he puts his cell phone in his pocket. Suddenly he changes his mind and pulls it back out. "I'll just make it a guys' night out," he says as he starts scrolling through his contacts list. Landing on his best friend Mike's profile, he presses Call.

Ring, ring, ring.

"Hey, Mike! What's up dude?" he says excitedly. "Yeah, not much here either. Hey, what do ya say we get a few of the guys together tonight? You know, a guys' night out." The smile sliding down now, he says, "Oh, you and your wife have plans, huh? Nah, it's okay, we'll catch up another time. All right, man, have a good one."

"That guy is whipped with a capital *W*," Anthony says out loud as his thumb scrolls in search of another friend. "Okay, Brian. He's the guy. Let me call Brian."

Ring, ring.

~ If Only ~

"Hey, Briannn. What's up, dawg?" Tony's smile drops as he hears the response from his friend. "Oh, oh, shoot! I'm sorry, dude. I didn't know you were on a date. Yeah, no problem. Let me let you go. Talk to you later."

"Okay, zero for two," Anthony says with a note of discouragement in his voice. "That's okay, we'll get something going."

Twenty minutes later and down to the last number he is willing to call.

"All right, man, another time. Have a good one," he says as he stares into the screen of his cell phone.

Pacing back and forth, Anthony's mind races as he tries to think of anyone who he can hang out with for the evening. Frustrated and with no other option coming to mind, he puts his phone away.

"Well, I'm going out one way or another." Determined to have a good time tonight, he forges out into the town alone.

After a couple of hours of dancing with no real connection made, Anthony retreats to the bar, where he is never turned down.

"What can I get you, dear?" the beautiful bartender asks.

"You know what? Make it a double of something strong. Surprise me." It takes all his strength to say the words.

"Rough night?" she says sympathetically as she scans over the bottles of liquor, searching for just the thing to pour.

"Not much of a night at all."

After some pouring and shaking, she slides the powerful concoction to him. "Here ya go. Hold on to your seat," she says.

He raises his eyebrows at her. "Really, what's in it?" But as she is about to reveal her secret, he says, "You know what? Never mind. I don't want to know."

Another hour and one more of the secret potions later, Anthony can no longer hold up his head. Out of mercy, the bartender lets him nap for a while before nudging him to settle up his tab.

"What, who...who's there?" he says as he tries opening his eyes.

"It's time to close up, dear. Wanna settle your tab?" the bartender says sternly.

"What?" He raises his head and looks around, spit connecting his mouth to the bar top.

"That's gonna be thirty bucks, sweetie, and here is a coffee to try and wake you up."

"Okay," he answers, thumbing through the bills in his wallet. "Here ya go."

Anthony can barely keep his eyes open as he drives.

"What in the world did she put in that drink?" he says out loud, hoping it will wake him up. "And why did I have two of them?"

~ If Only ~

Radio, he thinks to himself. "I'll turn up the radio. That'll help." Again he says it out loud as he continues to blink, fighting off the urge to doze away.

Swerving in and out of the oncoming traffic, Anthony is startled by horns blowing and pulls the wheel to get back on his side of the road. Turning the radio up louder, he decides to put down the windows and let the frigid air in. Coming to a stop at the red light offers momentary relief but also allows him to doze off. The driver behind him begins blowing his horn when Anthony doesn't pull off at the changing light.

"What? Okay, okay I'm going," he yells out the window as his right foot mashes down on the accelerator.

"Only a little ways to go," he says now with hope that the frightening ride will soon be over.

Eyes very heavy, mind drifting away, Anthony struggles more fiercely to stay awake but with little to no effect.

Only one more light to go, he thinks to himself as he sees it nearing. Dozing off again as he reaches the light, he doesn't notice that it has turned yellow and then red. He does not brake but rather keeps rolling into the intersection. He is suddenly on a crash course with a pickup truck coming from the street to his left.

The driver of the pickup, seeing his light turn to green, speeds up, thinking Anthony will stop. Then bracing for impact, he lays on his horn and slams on his brakes. The squealing brakes and horn finally wake Anthony, and he also slams on his brakes. Seeing the pickup just inches from his car, Tony is fully awake now and scared out of his wits. Breathing heavily and sweating profusely, he loosens his grip on the steering wheel and relaxes in his seat for just a moment.

A half hour later, finally home, Anthony walks straight to his bed and drops, falling fast asleep all at once.

10

Back at the Club

Anthony pushes through the crowd. He can see the bar in the distance, and he needs a refill.

This place is huge, he thinks to himself. So huge that each step he takes seems to bring him no closer to his destination, though he can still see it straight ahead. The music is loud, providing the dancers with plenty of energy. Song after song, he seems to know them all. Everyone is going all out, having a good time, dancing, drinking, talking, and laughing at tables. All have either been enslaved by the music or set free by it. Anthony finds it very chilly in the club, and as he looks around, everyone has goose bumps, but no one seems to be bothered by it but him. Finally he reaches the bar and looks up and down for the bartender, to no avail. Puzzled, he turns his head back to the dance floor when he hears from behind him, "What can I get you?" Turning back, he sees a beautiful young blonde leaning on the bar, waiting for his response. Having always fantasized about being a spy, he says, "A martini. Shaken, not—"

"Yeah, I got it. Actually I get that too much. Coming right up," she says. She begins to make his drink as he leans on the bar with his elbow and looks back onto the dance floor. His eyes catch another beautiful young woman who is walking straight for him.

"Here you go," says the bartender.

"Oh, thanks," replies Anthony as he turns to get his drink. When he turns back, the young woman is in front of him, which startles him, causing him to jump a little.

He quickly rebounds by saying, "I don't know if you are the sun or the moon, but you are definitely lighting up my life."

"Is that so?" she replies.

"So can I get you drink?" he says and turns to order one, but the bartender is gone. Looking bewildered, he turns back and shrugs to the young lady while pointing toward the bar.

"That's okay," she says. "Maybe later."

"So you'll be around later huh?" he asks smugly.

"Well, I did say *maybe*." She smiles.

"This place is great," he says, looking around. "You come here much?"

"I actually own it, so, yeah, I'm here a lot," she replies, sitting down on a bar stool. "You know, I can already tell I'm gonna like you."

"Really?" he says as he sits down.

"Yeah, there is just something about you. I can't quite figure it out, but I like it." She is now running her finger lightly up and down his forearm.

"What do you say we find a place a bit more quiet?" he says, his interest now piqued.

"I've got just the spot. Let's go." She takes his hand and leads him down a long dimly lit corridor. His mind now racing with thoughts, Anthony holds tight to the mysterious young woman's hand and continues to follow her, thinking to himself, *Beautiful woman, deserted place. What could be better?* Then he realizes that he doesn't know her name and he hasn't told her his.

"I'm Anthony," he says.

"Yes, I know," she bluntly replies.

Confused now, he is about to ask her what her name is when they reach their destination. She opens the door and turns to look at him as she seductively pulls him into the room. Inside he sees a large sofa in the center of a very large room. As she reaches the sofa, she sits down, slipping her feet out of her shoes and running her toes through the soft carpet. Pulling him down beside her, she starts running her fingers through his hair. Candles all around the room show off her beautiful features, and he can hardly believe his dumb luck.

"Comfortable?" she says softly.

"Very much so," he replies.

"Good. You are in for a night you won't soon forget." She continues exciting him. "Are you ready?" she asks.

"Oh yes," he quickly responds.

"Okay, turn 'em on," she says loudly as she pulls away and quickly stands.

Suddenly the large room is flooded with light, and Tony quickly closes his eyes. "What's going on?" he says as he slowly opens his eyes again, adjusting to the lights. To his surprise and amazement, the room is flooded not only with light but also with women, which, at first glance, excites him, but as he looks around the room, he notices they're all women he has gone out with before. He is surrounded by angry women who he has, at one point or another, dated.

"What is this?" he says as he tries to get up from the couch, only to be pushed back down by two of them.

"Sit down," they say. "You're not going anywhere."

The young nameless lady sits back down beside him and begins to explain.

"Anthony Edison, you have been brought here to explain your behavior to all of the women that you have jilted over the years."

"What?" Tony exclaims.

"I know," she says. "You were hoping for another cozy evening on the couch, huh? Well, that's not happening tonight."

"That's right, you pig!" another woman says.

Then suddenly they all move in closer, screaming and clapping their hands and waving their hands with their index fingers up in front of him while they shake their heads. Even though the whole room is in chaos, Anthony can hear each individual woman, their complaints registering loud and clear and releasing so many memories of his not-so-good past.

"One date and you are never heard from again."

"Got what you wanted and then hit the road."

"Juggling several women at once."

"You went out with my sister."

On and on they go. So many of these moments he'd not even given a second thought to when they happened. His eyes run back and forth, trying to take it all in but failing. Overwhelmed by them all, Anthony's mind begins to spin. Then suddenly all the sound is drowned out by a high-pitched ring. He looks toward the door of the room, and standing there by herself without saying a word is one woman, her head facing the floor. Instead of being angry, she simply looks hurt. Then the ringing is gone, and there is nothing.

Anthony wakes up in a pitch-black room covered in sweat. Trying to calm himself from the nightmare, he can only say one word.

"Adrianna."

11

Come with Me, Please

Anthony wakes to possibly the worst headache he's ever had. His bedroom curtains cracked open just enough to let in the blinding early morning sun that forces him to turn over. When he does, he sees out of his one squinting eye, as he raises himself up onto his left elbow, a small note on the nightstand. It reads, "Call me…for real this time. Adrianna." At the bottom, there is a small happy face and a small frowny face.

Oh man, my head is killing me, he thought to himself as he held it in his hands and eased himself back down to his pillow. Then he whispers, "If the club had hurt this much last night, I wouldn't have stayed as long."

Reaching back with his left arm, he picks up the note, raising it up into the air and reading it again. "But at least there is Adrianna…sweet little Adrianna," he says a little louder and with a smugness to his voice, until his head reminds him to keep the volume down. Looking away from the note with a puzzled look on his face, he notices that he is still in the clothes he wore last night, and in relief, he takes a deep breath.

Just then he is startled by his cell phone ringing. He sits up faster than he really should have, and he has to grab his head again, this time to make the world stop spinning. "No, no, no, stop!" he screams out. He frantically looks around the bedroom for the ringing phone. Not able to spot it, he has to get out of bed and search. Picking up his jacket from the chair across the room, he finds it in the pocket and finally gets the ringing to stop. Glancing at the caller name as he answers, he sees that it is Renee. Answering quietly, he says, "Renee, it's early, and on a Sunday no less. What do you want?"

"Well, hello and good morning to you too, dear brother," she says with a smirky tone.

"Come on, sis, cut me some slack. I have a horrible headache," Anthony says pitifully as he sits back down on his bed.

"No doubt destroying your liver a little more last night," she quips.

"Renee," he begs.

"Okay, okay, I'll ease up," she says with a little chuckle, enjoying torturing him just a little too much. "But only if you do me a favor," she says.

Trying not to sound as annoyed as he really is, Anthony says, "What kind of favor?"

With her squeaky timid voice, she replies, "Go to church with me this morning."

"Renee, hello, horrible headache, remember?" Anthony barks, no longer able to not sound annoyed.

"Well, excuse me for not scheduling my requests around your precious hangovers, but you know Sunday morning church kinda only happens on *Sunday* mornings," she snaps back.

Letting out a long sigh, Anthony calms down and thinks for a second, then responds, "Okay, but we haven't been to church since we were eighteen. Why now all of a sudden do want me to go with you?"

"Look, ever since Uncle Lou died, I just keep thinking." She stops and sighs and then grows quiet for a moment.

Anthony breaks in, "Renee, you are not Uncle Lou. Stop putting so much pressure on yourself."

Relieved he broke the short silence, she continues, "I know, I know, but I just can't stop thinking, thinking about Uncle Lou, about Mom and Dad. It's just a lot to process. And then yesterday at the store, I ran into Pastor and Mrs. Richards."

"Really?" Tony seemed surprised. "I haven't seen them for years. I mean, you know, except for the funeral and stuff."

"Yeah, I know," she says, "but anyway he asked if I would think about coming today. He said things were different now. You know, more people our age and stuff like that. He asked about you too. He said he thought we would like it better now." After another short pause, she says, "So what do ya say? Will you go with me? You know I hate going to new places alone, and this is kinda like new again."

Knowing he can never turn her down when she sounds so desperate, he gives one more try, albeit halfheartedly. "Renee, I'm not even dressed yet. I haven't eaten," he says as he walks through to his living room, not noticing that she is peeking through the blinds.

"I will get you something to eat on the way. Oh, and what you had on last night will be fine since it looks like you are still wearing it anyway."

Anthony looks down at his clothes, then around the room, spotting Renee outside his window smiling and waving. In defeat, he lowers his head and opens the door for her.

12

It's Off to Church We Go

Even though Renee had told Tony about the new church building on the way over, it still was a bit of a shock for him to see it. They both had many thoughts running through their heads during the drive.

"You sure about this, sis?" Anthony asked.

"Let's just give it a chance, okay?" she said.

"Okay," he said and tried to finish his breakfast quickly. One more sip of orange juice and he was ready to go.

"All right," he said. "I'm ready."

They both got out of the car and started across the parking lot.

"You gonna lock it?" Anthony asked with a disapproving look on his face, not wanting to walk any further until she complied.

"Anthony, we're at church," she snapped back.

"We don't know these people. Lock your car." He raises his eyebrows.

"Fine." She pushes the button on her key fob and waits for the beep. "Can we go now?"

"Yeah, I'm just saying. You're far too trusting," he says.

"You do not trust enough, but can we not argue today? I really want this to be a good experience. I really need it to be." She starts out scolding but is begging by the time she finishes.

As they get a little closer to the building, Pastor Richards spots them and smiles. He is at the door, greeting people as they come in. Anthony makes eye contact with him and smiles but is thinking to himself that he wished he could slip in unnoticed.

"I'm so glad you two could make it. Thank you so much for coming," Pastor Richards greets them with a smile that seems to take years off of his life.

"Well, sis here wrangled me up this morning, but it's good to see you too, Pastor," says Tony.

"He has no choice. If I asked him to do something, he can't turn me down," Renee says, smiling sheepishly.

Mrs. Richards hugs them both and whispers to Renee, "Thank you so much for coming." Then she pulls away and says jokingly, "These guys can't resist us. Wife or brother, either way it doesn't matter." Then she pulls away. "Well, you two, there is much to see and hear, so make yourselves at home."

As Renee and Anthony walk inside, they are like two little puppies let outside on a spring day. There are so many different sights and sounds. Their senses are overloaded.

Anthony says, "This is not at all what I remember this church to be."

"Yeah, I know. Look, you could have eaten here," Renee adds, pointing to a café serving breakfast foods and coffee.

There is a flurry of activity everywhere—children coming out of Sunday school classes, little ones looking for their parents while older children look to avoid theirs, people milling around, greeting friends and visitors, with many stopping to greet Renee and Tony. The sound of music growing louder is directing them to the auditorium, as well as the line of people, like lemmings, all headed in the same direction. As they are finally funneled in, they see all the sights that go along with the sounds they could hear. There is a band on stage singing songs ranging from classical hymns to contemporary Christian music. Several projector screens with ads running for the different ministries of the church line the walls and hang over the stage. Renee and Anthony find a seat and just take it all in, waiting for the service to start.

"When did this happen, Renee?" Tony asks.

"I don't know," Renee answers. "I'm just as shocked as you are."

At that, Pastor Richards catches up to them.

"I know this is very much different than you remember, guys."

"Yeah," Anthony says. "No one told me I needed a haircut. I guess because most of them have hair longer than mine."

"There's just so many people here. I mean, back then we had what, fifty or sixty?"

"I know. A lot can happen in what, ten or twelve years," Pastor says. "Look, give it a chance. The message is still the same—Jesus Christ and Him crucified."

Just then, the song leader stands up to the microphone and opens the service. "Hello, everyone, and welcome to City on a Hill Church."

Whispering, Pastor Richards leans closer and says, "I guess that's my cue to go. I'll see you after the service."

Renee and Anthony both say, "Okay."

With the last song and the dismissal of the service, the silence is broken, and the whole church seems to start chattering all at once. People are once again in a flurry of activity. Many more come to welcome Renee and Anthony. The band plays a few songs, but now with a lower volume. The twins start making their way to the door but are stopped several times along the way. Finally they make it out of the auditorium and are greeted once again by Pastor and Mrs. Richards.

"Thanks again for coming. You have no idea how much of an encouragement it's been to see you both," Pearl speaks up.

Renee grabs Anthony's arm and hooks hers around his. "Thanks for having us. Don't I have a good big brother for coming with me?"

"Yes, you do. You two have always been close," said the Pastor. "I am so glad we ran into you yesterday."

"Me too," Renee adds. "This has been nice."

As they continue talking back and forth, Anthony still feels out of place, and his eyes scan the crowd. He sees a few people he knows but most he doesn't. Then his eyes look across to an exit door on the other side of the vestibule, where he sees Adrianna. She is looking at him in bitter disappointment. He waves with his free arm, but she shakes her head and turns to go. Puzzled, Anthony turns back to his group to excuse himself and runs out to find her. Quickly moving across the parking lot, he sees her getting into her car and tries to catch up, but before he can, she drives off. He is left, standing among all the others who are trying to leave, watching her speed away.

≈ 13 ≈

1950: A North Carolina Prison

Tick, tock, tick, tock, tick, tock.

The ticking sound of the wall clock is deafening to Thaniel as he sits waiting for Edwin Marion to be escorted into the visiting room. Edwin, according to the newspaper in Thaniel's hand, is set to be executed in the morning for armed robbery and two counts of murder. The room is small and cold. The walls are painted gray, matching the skies outside, as if to mark the somber occasion. An hour has passed, with Thaniel sitting in front of a thick glass window waiting for Edwin to arrive.

"It must be very difficult to relax and simply visit anyone with this imposing environment surrounding you at all times," he whispers to himself.

Finally Edwin is brought into the room on the other side of the window. The look on his face says that it really doesn't matter who it is that has come to visit. He sits down quietly, with almost no expression on his face at all. They both reach for a phone receiver at the same time.

"Hello, Mr. Marion. My name is Thaniel. Thank you for agreeing to see me," Thaniel says calmly.

"You're welcome," Edwin says nonchalant. "You one of the victims' family?"

"Oh….no, no, I'm not," Thaniel replies, not expecting that question.

"Just figured you were looking to ask me for something before it's too late," Edwin responds.

Nodding as if the question made sense now, Thaniel continues.

"I see. No, sir, I have questions for you, but they're for your well-being." He holds up the newspaper and says, "I read the report of your coming exec…of your…of tomorrow's—"

"Of tomorrow's gassin'. It's all right. You don't have to say it if it is too much for you. Heck, it's too much for me, but I know it's only right," Edwin interjects.

"Yes, well, I'm just concerned as to whether you are ready to go or not," Thaniel says, sounding very much like a vacuum cleaner salesman.

Edwin, looking down at the Bible on the desk by Thaniel's hand, says, "You a preacher? What church are you from?"

"Well," Thaniel replies, "let's just say I travel a lot. I try to help people in a lot of different places."

"I figured you ain't from 'round here. People here are ready for me to die," Edwin says matter-of-factly, with no expression on his thin pale face.

"I see," says Thaniel, opening his Bible and then looking back up at Edwin. "I know you've done some bad things, Edwin, and it seems that you understand that you reap what you sow. There is nothing that can be done about that. I've come to tell you that Christ died for you, Edwin. God knew long before you were even born that you would do those things and that you would be here this very day. He still died for you."

"Just so you know, mister, it weren't supposed to turn out that way," he says. "It all happened so fast."

"I'm listening," Thaniel replies.

"In and out. We was supposed to be in and out," recalls Edwin as he stares right through Thaniel and into the past. "He just kept looking at me. The bank guard. I yelled at him and shook the gun in his face. I accidently squeezed the trigger, then that other man jumped on me, and when I fell on the floor, I… I did it again." He sat still and silent for a moment. "Then we was scared and ran for it. Didn't even take all the money."

Thaniel sat silently, contemplating how so many lives were torn apart in such a short amount of time.

"I didn't mean it, preacher. I swear. It weren't supposed to be like that. We didn't want nobody to get hurt. Ain't a day gone by I ain't been sorry for what I done," Edwin says, tears now slowly falling from his eyes. "Will you tell 'em I'm sorry? Please."

"I will, I promise," Thaniel says as he notices the prison guard looking at his watch. "Edwin, you can't undo it. It's too late, and tomorrow, well, you know. Wouldn't you like to give yourself to Jesus? Your whole heart? Right now, you can do that."

"I don't know. It don't seem right," Edwin says, now trembling as he scratches at the counter nervously. "I done a bad thing, and this town hates me for it. How can God still want me?"

With a heartfelt sigh, Thaniel continues pleading with Edwin. "Edwin, God loves you. He does still want you. He has never stopped wanting you. In 2 Peter 3:9, it says, 'The Lord is not slack concerning his promise as some men count slackness; but is longsuffering to us-ward, not willing that any should perish, but that all should come to repentance.' Edwin, do you understand that?"

Nodding slowly, Edwin replies, "Yeah I guess so, but it's too late for me. My life is over," he continues, putting his head in his hands.

"Are you familiar with the story of Christ's crucifixion, Edwin?" Thaniel asks.

"Yeah, a little, I guess."

"There were two men crucified that day with him. Jesus told one of them that he would be with him in paradise that very day, Luke 23:43. Edwin, it's not too late for you."

The guard returns, turns to Thaniel, and says, "Time for him to go' sir." Another guard reaches for Edwin to lift him from his chair. "It's time to go, Edwin."

"No, please. If only we could have a few more minutes," Thaniel says.

"I'm sorry, sir. He has to go," the guard replies, holding the door open for Thaniel to leave.

"Okay. Let me underline these verses." Thaniel hurries to underline the verses and hands the Bible to the guard. "Please give this to him. Tell him I folded the pages for him to read. Tell him it's not too late."

Thaniel looks once more at Edwin. Edwin turns back to look at Thaniel and then is taken out.

14

Why?

Anthony, now in disbelief and bewilderment, walks back to the church. Just as he makes it to the door, Renee is coming out.

"What's going on? Are you all right?" she asks.

"It's Adrianna. That was Adrianna," Tony says.

"What?" Puzzled, Renee asks, "Who was Adrianna?"

"Do you remember I told you I had been out a couple of times with a girl named Adrianna?" he says.

"Yeah. So?"

"Well, that was her," he says as they walk toward the car.

"Okay, well what happened? What did she say?" Renee asks.

"That's just it. She didn't say anything. She gave me this look from across the room and then left." They make it to the car and get in.

As she is pulling out onto the road, Renee says, "That just doesn't make any sense. Give her a little while and then call."

~ If Only ~

"Okay," Anthony says. Then his mind goes back to the note she left him about calling her. "Maybe she's mad because I didn't call this morning. Yeah, that's got to be it."

"Adrianna, please call me back. You know I've called several times. I'm sorry about this morning, but I didn't know you expected me to call first thing. I thought you just meant call. Anyway please call," Anthony speaks into Adrianna's voice mail.

Once he puts the phone away, Renee speaks up. "Tony, pacing is not gonna help. Just give her a little while."

"I know," he says as he sits down on the couch. "I just don't understand why she is so upset. I said I would call her, not that I would call as soon as I woke up."

"So has calling her back after a date been an issue?" Renee asks.

"You know me Renee," he says, defending himself.

"Yeah, I do," she responds as she now gets up from the couch and starts pacing. "Look, big brother, you go out with a lot of girls. You can't make a lot of girls happy, and if she has been out with you, then she probably figures if you don't call her back that you're also going out with others. Don't you think it's time to pick one girl and really date her?"

Anthony sighs. "Yeah, I know you're right, but actually when I woke up this morning and saw this note she gave me with her number on it, I mean, it didn't say much, but it just made me feel good. I thought maybe she is the one to seriously date. I was gonna call her this afternoon. I just don't understand why seeing me at church set her off."

Renee, still pacing, tries to talk it all through to figure out what upset Adrianna. "Okay, let's look at it again. You saw her from across the room, and she was already looking at you, right?"

"Yeah."

"And then you waved at her?"

"Yeah."

"Like, how did you wave? You didn't do something stupid. You know, some macho wave like this?" Renee points at him with her hands like two guns and gives her best chauvinistic smile.

"No. I just held up my right hand and waved," he said.

"Just you're right hand, not both hands like you're trying to flag her down or something?"

"No, you were holding my left arm, so I used my right one."

"Oh my gosh. That's it!" she exclaimed. "She saw me holding your arm. No, that can't be it. She wouldn't be mad that your sister was holding your arm.

Anthony sat silent for a moment thinking it all out.

"She does know you have a sister, right?" Renee asks disappointingly, as if she already knows the answer.

"Weelll…" Anthony says, wincing as he speaks.

"You mean to tell me that you never told her you have a twin sister?" Renee asked, now very disappointed.

"I don't know. Maybe. Maybe not. I don't, per se, remember specifically telling her. I mean we usually just go to the club or movies or something. I guess it never came up?" he says as if asking for her approval that it never came up.

"No wonder she's mad. She thinks you went out with her last night and then went out with me this morning. If it were me, I'd probably never speak to you again either," she scolds.

"I never meant to not tell her," he adds.

"I know what you meant. You meant to not get too attached to any one girl so you could see anyone else you might meet. Am I wrong?"

Anthony sighs and looks back at Renee for a moment, then turns away.

"It's very simple, big brother," she says. "If you think she is special, then you must treat her that way. You've got to be all in. Go call her again. Leave her a message. Tell her the truth, and then, for goodness' sake, let me meet her."

15

At Long Last We Meet

"I am so glad to meet you," Adrianna says.

Renee looks at Anthony, who, even though he is relieved that everything turned out well, looks like a scolded puppy.

"Yes, I'm glad too," Renee answers. "I'm sorry to have caused you distress."

"I am sorry," Anthony speaks up.

"I know, I know," Adrianna replies.

"Hi, my name is Kayla," the waitress says as she places paper coasters on the table. "I'll be taking care of you tonight. Can I get you guys started with something to drink?"

Anthony motions for Adrianna to go first.

"I'll have water with lemon please."

Then he nods to Renee.

"I'll have that as well."

"I'll have a sweet tea please," Anthony finishes.

"Very good," Kayla says. "I'll be right back with those."

After their dinners arrive, Adrianna asks if they mind if she prays over the table before they eat. Renee and Tony look at each other and give an awkward shrug of concession.

Adrianna lowers her head and begins, "Thank you, dear Lord, for your many blessings to us today. We thank you for your hand of safety and for the food you have given. Please, Lord, bless the hands which have prepared it for us. We pray that you might strengthen us by it that we may do your will. Thank you, Father, for your son, Jesus, for it is in his name that we ask these things. Amen."

"Amen."

"Amen."

Renee and Anthony are both looking at Adrianna when she lifts her head and opens her eyes. She looks at them both and then says, "I learned that prayer from my uncle. I always think of him whenever I pray."

Everyone begins to eat as they continue talking.

"I never knew you went to City on a Hill Church," Anthony says.

"No, I know you didn't. I guess you're not the only one who didn't tell some things," Adrianna replies. "But I've only been going for a few weeks."

"Oh, okay," Tony says.

"We grew up in that church—well, at least through our teen years. It was much smaller back then and on the other side of town. Our parents kept going after we stopped," Renee adds.

"Yeah, but we stopped when we left home." Tony paused for a few seconds. "It seems a bit different now. I mean besides it being bigger."

"Oh…how is that?" Adrianna replies.

"There were mainly older couples then. Sixties or seventies. Only a few couples younger than that and only three kids. Tony and I and another boy named Matthew," Renee says.

"I didn't like it then. It was always strict. You can't wear this, and you can't listen to that and cut your hair," Anthony says.

"I guess times have changed," Adrianna says. "I haven't found it to be like that now."

"Yeah, we were talking about that during the service," Renee says.

"How is everything? Can I get you anything?" the waitress breaks in.

"Everything is fine, thank you."

"Everything is good."

"Could you bring some napkins and maybe more bread?" Anthony asks.

"Of course, I'll be right back with that," the waitress says and walks off to complete her task.

"He loves bread, always has," Renee says as she leans in toward Adrianna. "Don't worry, I'll fill you in on all the gaps that he has left in his story for you."

~ If Only ~

Adrianna smiles.

"Hey, be nice over there," Anthony says.

"I am. I'm being nice to Adrianna." Renee laughs.

"So how did you start coming to City on a Hill Church?" Tony asks Adrianna.

"Well, a friend of mine has been inviting me for three or four years now," says Adrianna. "But I was always a nightclub girl, which, of course, is how we met."

"So what happened?" Renee questions.

"They had a huge outdoor party in October. They called it a harvest celebration. Hayrides, face painting, games—they really did a good job of it. They called everyone who had been saved in the past year and gave them a gift. They called the people God's harvest for this year. It was really nice."

"That does sound nice."

"Yeah, it actually does," Anthony adds.

"So I went to the church the next morning. It was different than any time I've ever been to church," Adrianna says.

"Really?"

"Yeah, well, you saw how it was the other day. I've never seen anything like that, and the sermon I felt like—" Adrianna pauses and looks back and forth at Renee and Anthony. "I felt like I was the only one there and that God was talking just to me."

"Wow," Tony says.

"Yeah, it was wow. He preached about not boasting of tomorrow, and I felt like God was calling me now and that I couldn't wait for another day."

Renee and Tony look at each other and then back to Adrianna.

"So when the preacher had the altar call, I went up and told him that God had called to me. He motioned for his wife, and she sat down with me. Long story longer, I asked Jesus into my heart that day."

"That's quite a story," Renee says.

"I guess that's why I got so mad at you, Anthony."

"I don't get it," he says.

"You and I have gone out on and off, and we're both nightclub people. We both have dated a lot of other people. When I saw you holding Renee's arm, I thought it was just another move in the game. I know because I've done it myself. Gone out with one guy today and with another tomorrow. Never call back. Just move on. I thought that's what you were doing to me. I don't want to be that person anymore."

"Well, that usually would have been spot-on but not this time," Anthony replies.

"Can I get you guys some dessert?" Kayla says, holding up the dessert menu. "We have some wonderful brownies, soft and gooey."

They all look at each other.

"No, I think we are all stuffed, but thank you," Renee answers.

"Hey, speak for yourself, sis," Anthony chimes in.

Renee and Adrianna, almost in unison, reply, "Well, maybe just a bite then."

16

1932: New York City

A quiet rain is falling, cold and steady. After nearly three years of the Depression, the United States looks like a dying nation. Nowhere is this more evident than New York City. The George Washington Bridge is uncharacteristically empty tonight except for a lonely figure pacing back and forth. Homeless for weeks now, she walks, destitute; everything she owns is on her back.

Thaniel is watching her closely. He knows what she is there for. He is hoping she will change her mind or at least that he can persuade her to. He has been appearing to her from time to time, giving her encouragement, trying to help her, trying to save her.

"Thaniel," he hears over his shoulder. Turning slowly, he sees his two best friends, Haniel and Jankiel.

"Thaniel, you know you mustn't—" he hears, but this time he cuts his friend off.

"I know, I know. I won't interfere with free will, but I have to do something," he says, looking back at his friends, who shrug their shoulders and nod an approval.

Appearing a safe distance away, Thaniel begins a slow walk toward the young lady so as not to startle her. "Are you all right, ma'am?" At the sound of his voice, she is startled, and seeing him, she begins to back away.

"Leave me alone," she screams into the rain.

"I'm not going to hurt you. I'm trying to help," Thaniel screams back.

"You can't help me. How can you help me? No one can help me," she replies, breathing heavily and staring out over the water.

"Just tell me what's wrong. Let me try," Thaniel pleads.

"Why, so you can fail me like everything and everyone else in my life has, including myself?"

Begging, he replies, "Can we just talk for a while? If you don't like what I have to say, I will leave you alone." Thaniel, now about thirty feet away, stops and leans against the rail and looks over to try to figure out what she is looking for. "What's your name? Why are you out here on such a stormy night?"

The young lady looks back at him for a moment without saying a word. The despair in her eyes grows with each breath she takes. "My name is Patricia," she says. "I can't take it anymore. I don't want to live this life another day."

"My name is Thaniel," he says, still leaning on the rail. Turning to her, he says, "I'm sorry things are bad for you right now. I won't tell you I understand because I don't. Everyone has their own problems. Do you think we could walk off this bridge and find somewhere else to talk? Some place dry?"

Patricia is immediately unnerved by this. "No, no. I'm not going anywhere with you," she says, now backing away from him.

Holding both hands out, he motioned for her to stop. "Okay, okay, I meant nothing by that. I was just trying to get you to come in out of the rain. Please just relax," he says, sitting down on the wet pavement.

Seeing Thaniel sit down, she stops backing away.

"Thank you," he says, talking in a more comforting tone. "Tell me, I know times are hard for most people right now, but why are you walking around on this bridge in the middle of a cold rainy night?"

"You mean besides having no place to go and no money?" she says sarcastically. "I've been out on the streets for a while now." She seems ashamed to be telling him this.

"I'm so sorry, Patricia, I know times are hard and money is scarce," Thaniel says, "but what does that have to do with this bridge?"

"Surely you know, or you wouldn't have come all the way out here," she says, turning her bitter face away from him.

Thaniel looks away too and takes a deep breath. Then turning back, he says, "I suppose I do, but why is this the answer? God loves you, Patricia. God loves you. He sent

His only true son, Jesus, to die for you, to die in your place so that He could give you life, not death."

Just telling her that made him feel so much better, made him feel like he was heading in the right direction and that this was going to turn out right. *If only she would believe that. If only she would receive God's love and His gift of salvation.* he thought as he looked at her, longing to make the decision for her.

Leaning on the rail and crying into her arms, she says, "He can't possibly love me. No one can.

"Oh, but he does, Patricia. Why would you say that?"

"I've done some horrible things. People make you do things. Men make you do things for money, for shelter," she confesses.

"Patricia, God forgives. He longs to forgive us. He waits for us until we are ready to come to him," Thaniel says, rain hiding the longing on his face. "Isn't there some family or friends somewhere that you can go to? Just to stay with until things get better."

"No," she breathes out, looking at Thaniel, exhausted, as if the word was too large to say. "The last time I saw my parents, we fought, and that's when I left. I tried to reach them a few months ago and found out that they had been killed when they walked in on a thief robbing their house."

"I'm so sorry, Patricia," he replies. "I can help you find a shelter to stay in."

"There is no shelter. There is no one. I have no one. Don't you see that?" she exclaims a little louder than she means to.

"You have Jesus, Patricia. He's waiting for you to want to come to Him." Every word gives Thaniel peace as it crosses his lips. "I know it may not seem like it when you have lost so much, but he will help you. You need only to put your faith in him."

"I don't feel like I have much faith left. Everyone and everything I know has let me down," she says despairingly.

At that, Patricia turns and leans over the rail. The rain subsides, and the clouds break enough to reveal glimpses of a bright full moon. She looks up to the silver light and then follows the beams back down to the murky Hudson River. Walking past Thaniel, she continues along the rail, looking over as she goes, as if searching for something.

Thaniel hurries to his feet, fearing the sudden burst of moonlight has undone his labor for the evening. "What's wrong, Patricia? What do you see?" he questions.

As if broken from a trance, she turns but at first does not reply. "I'm looking for the—" Deciding against finishing the thought, she stops, turning back to the water.

Thaniel, clearly unnerved by this change of events, seems frantic now, his eyes looking back and forth. Thoughts racing in his mind, he eases in as close to Patricia as he thinks he can without causing her to make a quick decision.

Haniel and Jankiel are watching this all unfold, but they are watching Thaniel, not Patricia.

"Patricia," Thaniel calls out, "Patricia, Scripture tells us that life and death are in the hands of the Lord. Please do not do anything rash."

She looks back momentarily, tilting her head softly to the side, showing her appreciation for his dedication to her this evening, then continues her search.

"Patricia, Christ has died for you. Call on Him now. He has prepared a better life for you," Thaniel proclaims.

Without turning, she stops and says, "I hope so. I cannot bear this one any longer." Turning back to Thaniel, desiring to lift the weight off herself, she bears the rest of her burden to him. "Sir, even in the horrible times, men have no mercy. They think only of themselves. They see a young actress looking for work, respectable work, and the only thing that stirs them is their basest appetites. They dangle food and money but only if their conditions can be met for the evening. They like to have the destitute at their beck and call. The starving will do many things…" she says, her voice trailing off. With this, she stops, as if she has found what she has been looking for, and now her eyes are fixed upon it.

Thaniel, desperate now, leans in a little closer.

"Thaniel, Thaniel," his friends call out.

Ignoring them, he continues to think, scrambling for anything. "I know man's sins are great, Patricia. The Bible says there is none good, no, not one, but God is good."

She begins to look at the railing now, feeling the rail and the fence with her hands.

"Patricia, there is none that seek for God, but He is seeking for you. Will you stop and seek for Him?"

"I have sought Him," she says.

"He is here. Now. All around us," Thaniel pleads.

Now looking for a way to get up onto the rail, she pauses and looks back at Thaniel. "I do not see Him, sir. I fear He no longer looks for me. Though I have not eaten for days, I can no longer take the food that is dangled before me. There is no work. I have no one to turn to," she says and begins to climb the rail.

Thaniel leans in closer, and Haniel and Jankiel reach for his arms to stop him.

"You have been kind, sir, but I can no longer be in this life." Looking Thaniel in the eyes, she falls backward into the light and then into darkness.

"Nooo!" he cries, reaching for her but cannot grab her for the strength of his friends.

And then there is silence, and he looks to see her purse leaning against the fencing of the bridge.

"We are sorry, Thaniel," his friends say, apologizing for stopping him and for what has happened. "You know it is not permitted that we interfere with their own desires."

Thaniel pulls his arms away from them angrily, staring down at her purse and simply breathing heavily.

After a moment, he calms himself and slowly reaches for her purse. Opening it, he reveals, among her meager possessions, a small Bible. It is the Bible he gave her several weeks before. He notices the ribbon bookmark placed at Romans 10. Verse 13 was underlined, "For whosoever shall call upon the name of the Lord shall be saved." Closing the Bible, Thaniel pulls out a small note, and unfolding it, he reads, "My name is Patricia Earlywine. I know this may seem cowardly, but I can no longer bear the pain of this life."

Folding the note and placing it in the purse again, he sets it back down in its place. Looking over the rail, he sees her body resting on a large rock, facing upward, waves crashing on her again and again.

"Thaniel, we are sorry," he hears from behind him. He says not a word, looking straight ahead he unfurls his wings and flies off, leaving Haniel and Jankiel alone.

17

Been a While, Huh?

The auditorium lights slowly brighten as the video comes to a close. Pastor Richards's voice breaks into the silence. "Thank you for playing that video for us," he says, nodding to the audiovisual team. "So there will be a short meeting after church today for anyone who would like to participate in this quarter's food drive. As usual, Jason will be heading that up, but he is having voice issues today from all the screaming he did at last night's hockey game. Pray for him. He hasn't yet surrendered his life to giving up worldly sports."

Laughing spreads throughout the church.

"No, no, I'm just kidding. Don't pray for him. He really should suffer for his sin."

Laughter again, this time a little louder, fills the air.

"No, I'm seriously just joking. We love Jason and appreciate so much his hard work on this project."

Pastor Richards, looking over to his wife, Pearl, sees her making a motion with her hand to wrap it up.

"Okay, so if you would like to help with this important project, whether it be to package or to deliver, please stay after for just a few moments and meet with Jason down front. Jason, put your hand up so everyone can see it."

Jason raises his hand.

"A bit higher, brother," Pastor says.

Jason stands quickly and waves and sits back down.

"Thank you, Jason. Now we will have the closing prayer and then dismiss."

"Lord, we thank you for the time of worship we've had today. May your message stay powerful in our hearts and move us as you would have us move. Bless the food that has been gathered and all those participating and receiving, and please keep us safe as we leave here today. Dear God, we love you for loving us first, for sending your son, Jesus, and your blessed Holy Spirit. We ask all these things in Christ's precious name. Amen and amen."

As the auditorium slowly empties, Renee makes her way down to the front, where about forty others are gathering. She sits in the third row back beside a couple of the other last ones to arrive. After another two or three minutes, Jason stands and turns to face the group. He begins to speak, and Renee cranes her head to see the face behind the weak, whispering voice. Once her eyes land on Jason, she is a bit surprised to see that it is Jason Westwood, whom she went to high school with. As he speaks, he scans the group, and coming to Renee, he immediately smiles and nods to her.

Though they were only friends in school, she is just a little embarrassed at the smile and feels her face getting warm.

Twenty minutes later, the meeting ends, and everyone makes their way out of the auditorium. Jason is left picking up his things as Renee walks down to meet him.

"Renee Edison. It's been a while. How have you been?" Jason strains to say, smiling.

"Jason Westwood. Wow, I did not expect to see you here, at least not heading up some big project."

Jason laughs and then winces, holding his throat. "Yeah, I usually kept to myself in school, so I guess I do look a little different now."

"It's a good look for you," Renee says as they start walking up the aisle toward the vestibule.

"Hey, are you in a hurry to leave? Would you like to get some coffee or something and talk for a bit? You know, catch up on life after school?" Jason asks as they reach the door.

"Oh, well, I don't know. Where did you have in mind?" Renee follows, walking through the door he opened for her.

"Well, if it will make the afternoon easier for you, we do have a café here at the church," Jason offers, pointing across the large open area to the sign for the small shop.

"Yeah, I know, this place has just about everything, doesn't it?" she responds.

"It's a small place. Just sandwiches and stuff, but it's nice. So what do you say?"

"Sure, let's go."

Lifting their heads after Jason's blessing on the food, they look out at the remaining activity in the church.

"I'm surprised so many people are here," Renee says.

"Yeah, Sundays are an all-day event for a lot of people," Jason replies. "There's always some group meeting or practicing, and, of course, we have Bible study on Sunday night."

"So how long have you been coming here?" Renee asks.

"Oh, let's see, about eight years now," he replies.

"Oh my gosh, these paninis are so good," Renee says after trying her first bite.

"Umm," Jason grunts as he is chewing. When he is finished swallowing, he says, "I know. They do a really good job here."

All through lunch, Renee kept thinking how different Jason seemed from their high school days. He was very quiet then and reserved. Now he is outspoken and seems so vibrant. She also noticed that there was no wedding ring on his hand but could have sworn she remembered him getting married several years ago.

"If you don't mind me asking, I thought I remembered hearing that you had gotten married. What happened?" Renee asked. "I see you aren't wearing a ring now."

Jason looked down for just a second, then motioned that they go for a walk. "I was married. She went home to be with the Lord about three years ago."

~ If Only ~

Feeling horribly guilty for asking, Renee replies, "Oh, Jason, I'm so sorry. I didn't know."

"It's all right. You couldn't have known," Jason breaks in.

"What happened?" Renee reaches for his hand.

"Well, um, she was complaining of a bad headache one morning, so she said she was going to take the day off to rest. When I came home from work, I found her. She was already gone. Coroner said it was an aneurysm."

"Oh my, I'm so sorry. I'm sorry you had to be the one to go through that," she says, tears welling up in her eyes.

"You know, for a while I kept thinking, 'If only I had stayed with her,' but the doctor said it wouldn't have mattered. God was just ready for her to go. You can't do anything with that. It took a while to wrap my head around, but we had a great time together, and God said it was time, so I'm okay," he said with a peaceful look on his face.

"Wow, I'm so proud of you for being so strong like that," Renee says.

"Well, I wasn't at first, but I'm okay now, so anyway, enough about me. How about you?" Jason says.

"I…I was just moments away from saying I do when my fiancé's girlfriend burst through the church doors and interrupted the service," Renee says with a matter-of-fact look on her face, which she followed with a chuckle.

Jason's jaw dropped, and he didn't say a word.

"Yeah, crazy huh?"

"Um…just a little. What did you do?"

"Turns out he was playing both of us," Renee says, slightly tilting her head. "When she found out about the wedding, she rushed over. Then she told the whole church full of people how he was treating us and that she was pregnant."

"Oh…really? I'm so sorry," Jason adds.

"What are you gonna do, right? I'm just glad she made it in time," Renee says.

"No kidding. Saved by the door, huh?" He shakes his head.

"It hurt then, but I can laugh about it now."

"Well, I'm glad for that. I hope you know that all of us guys are not like that," Jason says, almost asking.

"Yeah, I know. I just overlooked all the warning signs. Looking back, I don't see how, but anyway…" Renee says, smiling.

"Well, I guess we'd better get going. Gotta get ready for tonight."

"Okay. I'm so glad I ran into you. This has been nice," Renee says, touching his forearm.

"I'm glad too, and thank you for helping out with the food drive. See you next Sunday?" Jason asks.

"Yep, yep, next Sunday it is."

18

London 1880

As is so often the case, Timothy walks about in a bit of a daydream, or shall we say, night dream, in this case. He's excited that he has finally earned enough money to buy passage for himself and his beloved, Clara, to go to America. For such a long time now, he has worked hard and saved every farthing, biding his time until he had enough to show her that he could take care of her. He worked late every night, doing odd jobs, and toiled in the factory during the day. Both of them, being without any family and with times so hard here in London, had dreamt of the tales of promise and prosperity that awaits anyone brave enough to cross the Atlantic and take it for their own.

But tonight, the panic finally lifting, is not just another night. Tonight Timothy is ready, so ready to see his dreams come true, to touch them and taste them. Tonight he is to meet Clara for what she supposes is just another moonlit stroll to take away the cares of this life for just a little while.

But tonight is different, and he can't contain himself. A bright beaming smile is dripping off his face. His voice, so light and airy that it hides the years he has spent in poverty, cheers everyone along his path as he makes his way through the streets. But not everyone is happy for Timothy's good fortune, and his new clothes and bouncing stride are out of place in this part of town. The sun, now gone on this cold January evening, has taken with it the protection daylight has to offer, and Timothy, so wrapped up in his dreams, decides to take a shortcut through a dark alley.

"Well, well, well, what do we have here?"

Timothy is startled by this voice in the dark. He stops and looks carefully into the shadows when suddenly a figure appears.

"I think this one is a little bit out of place, boys. Whatever shall we do 'bout that?" the voice from the shadowy figure speaks again. The figure walks slowly toward Timothy, and behind him on either side, there are more figures appearing one by one. Ten in all appear and come closer step by step until they completely surround Timothy. Though he backs up slowly, they keep pace, not allowing him to leave the alley.

"Look, fellas, I don't want any trouble," Timothy pleads, his hand up and still trying to back up.

The apparent leader of the group walks around him, sizing him up. Stepping in front of Timothy, he pulls his cigarette from his mouth and flicks it away. Staring straight into Timothy's eyes and blowing out his last puff of smoke right into his face, he says, "No, I don't suppose you do." Reaching out and running his fingers under Timothy's lapel, he says in a deep, gravelly voice, "Well, you shouldn't have come down this alley." Then he gives Timothy a push back into the arms of one of his mates, who pushes him back.

"Clearly poor judgment on m-my part," Timothy stutters.

As the two men continue their discourse, Thaniel watches and listens from the back side of the alley, hoping Timothy will find his way out of it and that he won't have to get involved.

Oh, how I despise having to fight humans. If only they knew how difficult it is to hold back and not hurt them too much, he thinks to himself as he fakes a yawn.

Fearing that the gang will go straight for the kill instead of simply a mugging, Thaniel appears and calls out to interrupt things.

"Gentlemen, I'm sure we can come to some amiable solution here," he says, walking out into the light.

To which the gang leader replies so arrogantly as to not even turn about to see who it is that dares to speak, "This is not your concern, and you would be wise to forget you were ever here and be on your way."

Thaniel slowly steps closer. The sound of his footsteps says nothing but insolence to the gang leader. Thaniel stops when he finally turns to see who it is.

"Is there something wrong with you?" he says. "Are you a bit slow? Do I need to break this down for you? Beat it before you get yourself hurt. What are you doing out here tonight anyway?"

Calmly Thaniel replies, "Oh, I'm just out doing the Lord's work tonight."

"Oh, here we have it, boys," the leader says as he looks around to all his gang. "Preacher man out tonight. Gonna try to soft talk us into changing our minds." Then he turns back to Thaniel and says, "Well, preacher man, we don't need to hear anything from you and your wimpy God."

As Thaniel takes a couple more steps, he says, "Oh, you would be very surprised at my God's power. And maybe a bit surprised at mine."

The gang leader nods at two of his men, who then roughly pin Thaniel's hands behind him. Then the leader grabs Timothy by the collar and turns back to Thaniel and says, "You see, now you've challenged me before me lads here. I think you and our little dandy here are gonna have to pay for it." He nods again as he punches Timothy in the stomach. Two of the gang members grab Timothy's arms as the leader prepares to hit him again. Behind them, the five members converge on Thaniel, who, faster than sight, takes the two who hold his hands and slams their heads together like a pair of cymbals. Then holding on to them, he spins himself, using them to knock out the other five as well. With seven men on the ground before the leader could throw the next punch, Thaniel runs forward and grabs his arm, swinging him around and sending him crashing into the building to their left. As the leader hits the ground, the two men holding Timothy look at each other, then drop his arms and turn to run, but Thaniel is instantly behind them. Thaniel grabs them both by the collar, lifting them off the ground. Looking straight into their terrified faces, he says, "Remember what you've seen here, and when you wake up, change your ways." With that, he slams both of their heads together and then throws each one against a building, one on each side of their leader. Just as the last two hit the ground, Timothy raises himself up, coughing and surprised, the flowers he bought for Clara still in his hand.

Thaniel reaches for his hand and says, "Looks like the path way suddenly opened up. Let's go."

Timothy, shocked, says, "What in the world just happened?"

Thaniel raises an arm and says, "God has given us a great victory, young man. We must give Him our thanks and praise His wonderful name."

Not really very grateful at all, Timothy replies, "Yeah, okay, um well, Preacher, I do appreciate your help, but, um, as far as I can see, God hasn't been on my side for a long time." Then he starts checking his pockets. "No, no, no, no, where is it? Where is it?" Then he starts panicking and looking around on the ground.

"What is it, friend? What's wrong?" Thaniel says.

"The ring. The ring. I was on my way to propose to my girl, Clara, when I ran into those guys," Timothy barks out.

Thaniel peers into the darkness. Spotting the ring, he picks it up and hands it to Timothy. "Look at this, my friend. God has given you a great victory."

"Look, Preacher," Timothy says as he takes the ring, "I know you mean well, but in case you're new to England, we've been in a terrible depression for a long time. I've worked hard for little money for many years to be able to propose tonight. God hasn't answered any of my prayers. He's left me to do it all myself." With that, he puts the ring back in his pocket and thanks Thaniel again and turns to walk away.

"But, young man, surely you can see how God has helped you along the way. Surely you can see what He's done tonight," Thaniel says.

"Yeah, I mean, you did well, Preacher, using the icy street and the gang's overanxiousness to your advantage. I do thank you, but as for God, I don't know." Shaking his head, he turns again and walks away.

In disbelief, Thaniel just stands and watches him leave.

19

Thaniel's Solace

Thaniel, needing time to reflect, has chosen a quiet part of the world and has rested himself on a cloud. The air is still, and all around him is only white fog. He is overwhelmed by the thought of the apathy of so many Christians of today, of so many people in the world in distress, of so many going their own way and so few going God's way. He sits alone like many times before, but this time, he is not alone. His friends wait for him far off so as not to disturb him. After a long while has passed and he has gathered his thoughts, he rises to pray. Standing straight, his head and hands lift to heaven.

> Holy, holy, holy. Thou art God the Creator, the Beginning and the End, the Father, the Saviour and the Holy Spirit. Amen.
>
> If only I could do enough to make you proud,
> could turn their hearts to yearn for things above
>   these clouds.

My raptured joy would cause my voice to sing out loud.
If only I could do enough to make you proud.

If only man could see the error of his ways
and understand how fragile his life is and of few days.
If only he would look above and give his creator all the praise.
If only man could see the error of his ways.

If only sin would show its tarnish instead of sparkling in man's eye.
Maybe then he'd kneel and pray, and God would hear his cry.
Then fear would never grip his heart when he's about to die.
If only sin would show its tarnish instead of sparkling in man's eye.

If only every eye was opened and all the world could see the truth.
Satan has been pulling them apart every moment from their youth, and Christ alone has the power to rescue.
If only every eye was opened and all the world could see the truth.

If only the world would turn their hearts and come to God

~ If Only ~

> If only they would walk the straight and narrow, not the broad.
> If only they would know God's love, they'd fall down in awe.
> If only the world would turn their hearts and come to God.

After prayer, Thaniel stands for a moment, not making a sound, his head lowered, his eyes closed, Haniel and Jankiel still watching.

"Is he all right?" Jankiel says as if Haniel is sure to know.

"Yes. I think so, but I am still concerned. As you already know, he spends a lot of time alone reflecting. This time, however, he seems more troubled than I recall ever having seen," Haniel replies, not taking his eyes from Thaniel.

"Let's go to him then," Jankiel says, moving forward.

Haniel reaches his arm out to stop him.

"We must not interrupt unless there is no other choice."

"Then what shall we do?"

"Wait."

After a bit longer, Thaniel lifts his head and eyes and turns to face his friends, giving them a direct stare. Then he moves toward them and immediately is there with them.

"You two don't have to follow me all the time. I am well," he says, giving them a look with both eyebrows raised.

"You knew we were here?" Jankiel asks.

"Of course he knew," Haniel quips, then turns to Thaniel. "You're not well, my friend. You are much too discouraged."

"I am concerned about these people, that's all," Thaniel replies sternly, motioning toward the earth.

"We are all concerned," his friends say in unison, looking at each other, surprised they spoke at the same time.

Sighing, Thaniel says, "I know. I know you both are. I know we all are. I just don't understand why I can't help anyone no matter how hard I try."

Thaniel's friends step closer, each of them placing a hand on one of his shoulders. Jankiel looking at Haniel, speaks up. "Thaniel, my friend, you are taking this much too personally. We are not responsible for making them accept Christ as Savior. We can only advise, encourage, and help them. You know that," he says tenderly.

Thaniel lowers his head and then begins shaking it slowly. "I know that." Then he breathes out a weary sigh. "What am I doing wrong? I have tried to immerse myself in their world as much as I can, tried to feel their life, tried to understand things from their perspective. What am I missing?"

Haniel lifts Thaniel's head as he continues. "You are not missing anything. There is no other angel that tries harder, that loves people more than you. They are God's creation, but you love them as if they were your own. You do anything and everything that you can. You give everyone that you care for the best opportunity to know God, but that's where it must end. You have to let it end there, Thaniel. Trusting God, accepting Christ, believing in the Holy Spirit—it must be their decision. Brother, you have to accept that."

~ If Only ~

"I know, I know," Thaniel says, reaching out to his friends, leaning in and drawing them close so that all three heads are touching as if in a football huddle. "It's just that I know the majesty of God, the splendor of His world, His home—our home. I know how wonderful all that we have is and how we enjoy it all. I want them to enjoy it too."

"We all do, Thaniel. We really do," Jankiel says as he slowly breaks the huddle.

"Speaking of our home," Haniel adds, "it's been far too long since you have been there. Come with us now, brother. See the Father. See all the angels. See the saints. See and hear everything. Feel God's love and power again." He reaches out and held Thaniel's shoulder. "You need this. Come with us, and when you come back, you will be reenergized."

"Come, Thaniel, you won't regret it. Home will help. God will help," Jankiel softly speaks.

Thaniel looks down toward the earth in anguish over what to do. After a short moment, he looks back to his friends. "All right, maybe you're right," he says, sighing. "I will come."

The three angels stand silent for another moment, looking at each other. Then all together turning their faces toward heaven, they stretch out their wings and jump up away from the cloud. Higher and higher they fly, from the bright blue sky into the black starry sea and beyond. Higher and higher, faster and faster. Within moments, they can see ahead the unmatched brightness of their home. The glitter and sparkle of the world that is always new, always perfect. Then they hear the shouts of praise and joy, the cheers, the singing. They hear the multitudes all crying out in unison, "Holy, holy, holy is the Lord God Almighty."

20

Let's Hit the Slopes

"Oh my gosh," Renee says as she hugs Jason's sister, Jennifer. "Jason said you were coming today. It's been so long. How have you been?"

"Good, good, I've been good," Jennifer replies, squeezing Renee so hard she almost picks her off the ground. "So how 'bout you?"

They step back away from each other, both smiling an at-home smile.

"I'm doing great. Your brother has been working me very hard on the weekends, though," Renee says, grinning at Jason.

Jennifer looks over at Jason, puzzled.

"The food drive. That's how we ran into each other," Jason clarifies.

"Oh, okay," Jennifer adds. "So, Renee, when are we gonna get together and relive the old days in drama class?"

"Well, we can't do it next weekend. That's the food drive drop-off day," Renee says, nodding at Jason.

"That's right," he adds.

"Oh, oh, I got it. You should come with us on our yearly ski weekend in three weeks!" Jennifer says excitedly.

"Ski weekend?" Renee questions, looking back and forth between Jennifer and Jason.

"Yeah, that's a good idea, sis," Jason says. "Yeah, for the last few years, our parents and brothers and sisters have all been renting this huge cabin up at the ski lodge. Some stay all week, but Jen and I usually just make a weekend out of it."

"You should totally come, Renee. It'll be fun. I'm sure Mom and Dad would love to see you," Jennifer pleads.

"But won't I be in the way? I mean, it is a family thing, right?" Renee asks.

"Nah. It's not anything formal like that. We all just go to have a good time together," Jason reassures.

"Well, all right, that does sound fun. Hey, listen, I've got to run. Jason, I'll see you next Sunday, and, Jen, I'll see you in three weeks," Renee says, backing toward the door.

As soon as Renee is gone, Jennifer turns to Jason with a big grin on her face.

"You just used me, didn't you?" she says laughingly.

Jason has a fake puzzled look on his face.

"I….I don't know what you're talking about," he says, trying not to smile.

"You do so," she replies, her eyes as big as basketballs and her face lit up like the Fourth of July. "I didn't realize it at first, but then I noticed you were just hanging back letting me do all the talking."

Jason is now trying to push it off, fumbling with papers and things in his hands and starting to blush a little.

"Oooh yeah! You used me to ask Renee out on a big ole date weekend in the mountains." She is now laughing out loud. "You are the same scared nerd you were in high school. This is hilarious!"

"Okay, whatever," he says, smiling. "It worked, didn't it?"

"Like a charm. Just let me know when you're ready to propose, and I'll see if I can work up a good one for ya," she says, still smiling.

"Ha-ha, very funny."

"Oh my gosh. After the breakfast we just had, how do you expect me to learn how to ski?" Renee says, holding her stomach as if to keep from exploding.

"Don't forget, there's also tubing and snowboarding," Jason says, trying to ease any pressure she may be feeling to keep up.

The snow is still falling but only lightly. A cold sun is trying to break through the sky, revealing patches of blue. Flakes sparkle on the tree limbs, rocks, and everywhere that the sun reaches. The air is cold, but still, people dot the mountainside between hills, trees, cabins, and the lodge.

Everyone's breaths linger in the air like tiny vaporous clouds, floating by and then disappearing. Renee and Jason walk out of the cabin into a winter wonderland.

"I'd like to try a little of all of them but maybe more of the tubing," she says with a childlike grin on her face.

As evening comes on, string lights begin to glow all over the mountain, and everyone seems to be in slow motion. A soft golden glow slides across the frozen resort. There are still a multitude of people going here and there, but it all seems quiet and relaxed. Thaniel has joined the activities, going as just another happy guest at the lodge. He stands in line on the snow tubing hill behind Jennifer, who is behind Renee and Jason. As Renee sits down into Jason's lap on the double tube, he helps her settle into place, and then they are into another speedy, giggly trip down. Just as Jennifer prepares to take her place, Thaniel speaks.

"They make a nice-looking couple, don't they?"

Jennifer looks at the two of them sliding into the pool of people at the bottom of the hill.

"They both have had some hard moments in their lives." She looks back at Thaniel. "They're not a couple, though. I know he wants to be. Not sure what she wants yet."

Resting into her own tube, she speeds away after them. At the bottom, Jennifer decides to call it a day and leave Renee and Jason to themselves.

"Okay, guys, that's enough for me today," Jennifer says as she walks off toward the cabin.

Renee and Jason drift away from the crowd into the soft glow and long shadows.

"You know, this has been the best day I've had in a long time," Renee says. "Thank you for inviting me."

"Well, I'm glad, and to be honest, I haven't had a day like this in a long time either."

Noticing a nostalgic look on Jason's face, Renee asks, "Do you think you'll marry again?"

"I hope so," he says, thinking back to his time with his wife. "You know, Natalie and I had a good life. We were a good fit. We did everything together, and I think we only had maybe one or two fights. Most people probably wouldn't have even called them fights. We worked, played, traveled, worshipped. We did everything together."

"So you had the fairy tale?" Renee asks.

"Yeah, I did."

"Can you even do that again?"

"Yeah," he says with a determined look on his face. "I'll have the fairy tale, or I won't have anything."

After a quiet moment, Jason asks Renee, "How 'bout you?"

"I never had the fairy tale."

"That's not what I mean. Can you go that far again? Can you trust someone that much again?"

"I tell you what, if it feels like a fairy tale, yeah."

They come to a bench in a quiet spot and sit, looking up at the stars.

"Can I confess something?" Jason asks, afraid to look at Renee.

"Yeah, of course. I mean, I guess. You didn't kill somebody and bury them in your yard, did you?" she says, trying to lighten his mood.

He smiles and laughs a little. Turning toward her, he says, "I crushed on you in high school, but I was always too scared to ask you out."

"Are you serious? I'm sorry. I didn't know. I was kind of oblivious then," she says apologetically.

"Well…" he says, drawing the word out for several seconds.

She turns her head and tilts it slightly, trying to figure out what he means.

"I used Jennifer to get you up here so I could have some time with you," he says, embarrassed. "She says I'm still the same scared nerd."

Renee is now thinking to herself, *Should I be flattered or scared?* She takes a couple breaths, then holds his hands in hers. "This has been a wonderful weekend, and if I am to be honest with you, I kinda thought of it as a date also. You made it easy because you didn't ask, and I could just be here and see how things would be."

She takes a couple more breaths and then looks him in the eyes. "I really could go for a fairy tale right about now."

Then she leans in and gives him one soft kiss. "But let's go slow so neither of us gets hurt."

Jason smiles, and they walk back to the cabin to meet up with his family for dinner.

21

I Never Knew

"Benjamin Ingles PLC," Tony reads the name off of the plaque at the front door of the lawyer's office, making a stiff body motion with a silly face.

"Yes, I'm sure he looks and acts just like that," Renee playfully scolds.

"Too much?" Tony asks, not really concerned about the answer.

"Yes, but I liked it. I couldn't let the opportunity to harass you pass, though," she replies, smiling a Cheshire cat smile.

Holding the door for her, Tony adds, "I know. Let's go."

Walking in to the conference room, Renee and Tony are puzzled. Mr. Ingles sits at the head of the long conference table, which they expected. However, they are taken back by the two people sitting on the side opposite them. Two twenty-something women sit patiently, waiting for the meeting to start. They seem just as confused to see Renee and Tony.

Clearing his seventy-year-old throat, Mr. Ingles begins to speak. "First of all, let me begin by thanking you all for coming. I know there must be a lot of questions, but if you will bear with me, everything will make sense shortly." Handing a packet to each of the four attendees, he continues. "As you all know, we are here to discuss the last will and testament of Louis Hamilton. What you may not know is that besides being his attorney, I am also one of Louis's closest friends."

Everyone is really confused now, looking at each other, shrugging their shoulders.

"Louis and I went to school and college together, and I actually introduced him to his wife, Virginia." Mr. Ingles pauses for a moment. "I know it may not have seemed like it, but Louis was a very loving man."

At that statement, all the others at the table sat back with a startled look on their faces.

"It's true." He continues, "He loved Virginia very much and treated her like a queen, and she was very good to him. When he lost her, though—" Mr. Ingles pauses again. "He was not the same after that. The one thing he wanted more than anything else out of life he denied himself because he couldn't bear to have it without her."

"What was it that he wanted?" Renee asks what everyone else wants to know but wouldn't ask.

"He wanted family, Renee. He wanted all of you but just couldn't do it without Virginia. He mourned her with his last breath."

The room fell silent for what seemed like days.

Bringing everyone back to the purpose of the meeting, Mr. Ingles speaks. "That's where you all come in. So let me introduce everyone and clear up all of this mystery." Looking toward the two young ladies, Mr. Ingles motions with his left arm toward Renee and speaks. "Girls, this is Renee and Anthony Edison. They are Louis's sisters' children." Mr. Ingles is now looking toward Renee and Tony. "And this is Sarah and Jessica Reynolds. They are Virginia's sisters' children."

"Oohhs" fill the room as everyone suddenly understands more than they have since this all began with Louis's passing.

"With all of your parents gone on now, you four are Louis's last remaining family. Although he failed in getting to know each of you, and believe me when I say he did regret that, he has named you four his heirs. Now Louis still owned 80 percent of his company, with twenty percent belonging to other shareholders, which means that now each of you owns 20 percent of Hamilton Windows and Doors."

Mr. Ingles directs them all to open the packets he has given them and then continues. "Now you may or may not know that Hamilton is the nation's largest window and door company. Louis left explicit instructions on how to run the company on an interim basis until all of you have had time to determine if anyone or all of you all interested in running the company. So in the coming months, there will be much to learn about, but suffice it for me today to tell that today you will each walk out of here with a sizeable sum as a first draft of your inheritance. Louis also has paid for financial guidance for each of you to help with all of this."

With everyone now sufficiently flabbergasted, the room is filled with chatter.

"Please, please let's wrap things up for today. Before we get into the disbursements, I just want to add that though he did not know how to show you, Louis loved you all very much."

"Wait, wait. I don't understand. Why didn't he just help our parents all these years so they didn't have to struggle so much?" Tony asks with a tone that was a bit harsher than he intended.

"Well, actually, he helped them more than you know, but your parents, being the people they were, would only accept help, not a windfall."

Everyone looks around at each other, once again trying to grasp the meaning in all of this. Renee speaks up once more.

"Why did we not know about Sarah and Jessica?" Then looking at them, she asks, "Did you guys know about us?"

Almost in unison, they respond, "No," as they shake their heads.

"Neither of your parents had ever met, as far as I know, so it's possible that it's just as simple as Louis never having shared that information with anyone. I can't answer as to why. Please remember, his whole life, his whole being was dramatically altered when Virginia died. He was never the same man again," Mr. Ingles shares. "I do believe that it would make him happy to know that you would meet and even get to know each other. Of course, there is no such stipulation in the will so that will have to be up to you four, but if I were you, I would at least talk and try anyway."

To which they all agreed with a silent nod.

"I know this is all a bit much to take in. I want you all to know that Louis has already paid me financially and with a lifelong friendship, so I am here to help guide you in adjusting and adapting your lives to make all of this become a positive change in your lives. Now let's get the documents signed and get you guys all settled."

22

A New Day

Renee is driving home after another stressful day at work. Although the drive is fairly short, it seems horribly long today. Every stoplight feels like an overwhelming burden. Six radio station changes in only four minutes and nothing is satisfying to her. A beautiful cloudless afternoon, which would normally be her favorite thing, brings her no comfort. The past few weeks have all seemed like a whirlwind, and she has so many thoughts fighting for her attention. Finding it all hard to manage, she rests her head in her hands while she is stopped at an intersection.

Beep, beep.

The sound from the car behind Renee startles her into looking up at the now-green light.

Beep, beep, beep. Now two more cars join in.

"All right already. Geez, it couldn't have been more than a few seconds," Renee barks, looking into the rearview mirror as she pulls through the light, which is now turning yellow.

Back at her apartment, Renee is much the same, flipping through channel after channel, not satisfied with anything. Turning her TV off, she sits with her head in her hands. Her eyes welling up with tears, she softly sobs as she whispers. "Why am I like this? Why can't I be happy?"

Taking a few deep breaths, she sits back against the sofa and wipes her eyes. Staring at the remote on the coffee table for a moment, she swipes it up in disgust and turns the TV back on. Channel after channel, nothing is right. News, sports, movies, sitcoms—she continues to surf until finally she lands on a church program. Thoughts begin to swim out of control all through her mind until suddenly one clear thought rises to the top, and she blurts it out, "Mrs. Richardson."

I wonder if she is at church now. Nah. Why would she be? she thinks to herself.

"It doesn't hurt to go and see, right?" she says out loud, justifying a drive across town as she grabs her keys and rushes out the door.

Walking up the church sidewalk, Renee is having second thoughts. Scanning the few cars in the parking lot, she thinks to herself, *I don't know if any of these are her car.*

Once inside, she sees only a few people floating around, and she decides to ask one of them if they have seen Mrs. Richardson.

The young man wiping tables in the café answers, "Yes, I think so. Probably in her office. Next to last door on the left at the end of that hallway." He points across to a dark hallway on the other side the open area.

As she passes by the auditorium, the faint strum of a guitar and the muffled sound of a voice seep out from the beneath the door. Overhead lights come on one by one as she makes her way down the hall. Looking ahead, she sees a bright glow pouring out from the open door near the end of the hall. Knocking on the frame, Renee watches Pearl Richardson lift her head.

"Hello, dear, come on in. It's so good to see you. How are things?" Pearl gleefully asks.

"Fine, I guess. I don't know. Just wanted to talk. I wasn't sure if you'd be here. I took a chance and drove over," Renee responds almost apologetically.

"I'm glad you did. Come on in, dear, and have a seat."

Renee steps in slowly and sits down in a chair across from Pearl's desk. Still looking at her laptop screen, Pearl says, "I'll be just a moment, dear, Let me finish this before I forget."

Renee nods in compliance.

"Hmmm, hmmm, hmmm," Pearl hums as she types the remainder of an e-mail and clicks Send. "Done," she says as she walks around her desk and sits in a chair closer to Renee. "You know, I'm always amazed at how God works things out."

Renee tilts her head inquisitively.

"I wasn't planning on being here tonight, but David wanted to practice the song he's been writing—you know, the one from the store a few weeks back?"

Renee gives an "aha" look of remembrance.

"So rather than to be home alone, I came in to do a few things." Then she reaches out and touches Renee's hand. "But I think the real reason I was supposed to be here was to talk to you."

"Has that ever happened before?" Renee asks.

"You'd be surprised. I can make plans to be here, and David and I can be the only ones here for hours. Then other days happen like this, and it usually proves beneficial. So what's going on? Let's talk."

Renee, confused and nervous, sits back and takes a deep breath.

"I don't know really. Everything has just changed since Uncle Lou's funeral." She sits and thinks for a moment. "I feel on edge all the time, and I think, or I guess overthink, everything," she continues.

Pearl, careful to listen well before speaking, simply says, "All right."

"You know I'm glad I started coming here again. I've enjoyed the services and even helping with the food drive. Reconnecting with Jason has been a good thing too. I just thought I'd feel better about things by now."

"So what? Things are not right?" Pearl asks softly.

~ If Only ~

"I…I worry a lot about…you know, when it's time to go, to die." Renee nervously gets up, looking down at the floor. "I just don't feel like I have the peace that everyone keeps talking about."

Pearl stands and walks around to the shelf in the corner and picks up her Bible. Walking back, she pulls her chair close to Renee and sits back down.

"Okay, so what you are saying is, you feel like you are doing all the right things, and yet you don't know why you still feel like something is wrong?" Pearl asked.

"Yes, exactly."

"I know you have heard a lot of scripture, but let's go over some anyway, okay?" she says, looking over at Renee, who nods in agreement.

"I think the best thing to do is start from the ground up and establish where you are in the scheme of things. So…," Pearl says as she turns her Bible pages. Stopping in the book of Romans, she says, "Romans 3:23 says, 'For all have sinned and come short of the glory of God.' So that means that you, me, and everyone else ever to have sinned do not measure up to God, right?"

Renee replies, "Okay," while nodding.

"The first part of Romans 6:23 tell us that for our sin, our wages are to be death. We all die, though, right? So of course that is speaking of spiritual death, eternal death. So we are all sinners and are worthy of eternal death. You still with me?"

Renee, following along with her on the page, says, "Okay, I'm with you."

"Okay, let's move on. So we are sinners, and God is righteous. How can we be righteous that we may be like him and be with him eternally?"

Renee answers, "I guess going to church and being good to people and helping others. You know, stuff like that."

"Well, that's where the problem comes in. You see, that would just make us a sinner doing good things. James 2:10 tells us if we keep the whole law and yet offend in only point, just one sin, that we are guilty of all," Pearl adds as she is turning the pages to show Renee.

Renee, reading and processing, sits back in her chair and sighs, frustrated. "So all this is for nothing? Then what about Jesus?" she says.

"Now you are getting it. Jesus is the answer. I mentioned the first part of Roman 6:23 a minute ago," Pearl says and begins turning back. "Let's see the second part…Here it is: 'But the gift of God is eternal life through Jesus Christ our lord.'" Pearl sits back in her chair. "Look, dear, you and your brother were good kids. We failed you. Our church was stiff and sometimes rude. We turned you away without meaning to. You sat right under good preaching and missed so much of it because love was missing from the equation." Leaning back on her knees, she turns her Bible to Isaiah 64:6. "Isaiah says that our righteous acts are like filthy rags. We're all dirty, Renee. We are not fit to enter God's house, so we must be cleansed if we are to enter. That's where God's gift comes in. King David believed that God would send a Savior. He knew that only God could cleanse him. In Psalms, he wrote, 'Wash me and I shall be whiter than snow.'"

Renee looks up at Pearl. "So what do I need to do?"

"You need only to accept that what Jesus has done for you: His life, His death, His resurrection—all the things you have heard about before, right?" Pearl raises her eyebrows to Renee.

Nodding, Renee says, "Yes."

"You need to understand that God sent Jesus, His only true son, perfect and holy, to suffer our eternal death for us, for our separation from God. Jesus took our place, and though He did nothing wrong, He died a sinner's death, and God, His Holy Father, saw Him as one of us—a sinner. But Jesus was not a sinner, and so death could not hold Him, and He rose from the dead and now is back with His Father." Pearl pauses for a second and then asks, "Are you still with me?"

"Yes."

"We must recognize that all Jesus did for us is the only thing that we have to break the separation between us and God. He is the only bridge available for us to cross. When we see that we need him and when we cry out to Him, He will save us. Then when God looks at us, He will no longer see us as sinners but as His own dear son." Turning to Romans again, Pearl shows her one last passage. "Look, Renee, at Romans 10:9–13." Paraphrasing, Pearl adds, "If we confess that Jesus and all He has done for us is what we need because we are sinners, if we trust Him and in His work and believe all of this in our hearts, if we call on Jesus, He will save us. That's what you are missing."

"I've never done that," Renee responds.

"If you are ready from your heart, you can do it now. You need only pray and call out to God," Pearl adds.

"Will you help me?" Renee pleads.

"I will, but you really don't need me. Just think of what I've just told you. Tell God you believe and that you know you are a sinner. Without Him, there is no hope for you. Ask Him to let Jesus's work on the cross be your salvation and take away your sin. Ask Him to accept you as one of his own."

After prayer, they stand, and Pearl hugs Renee, tears streaming from her eyes. "You have no idea how long I have prayed for this day, dear."

Renee, tears of her own welling up, says, "You've been praying for me?"

"For this moment, and here we are. Let's go tell David."

They walk toward the door, and Pearl turns off her office lights. Walking down the hallway, lights begin to turn on for them. Reaching the auditorium, they slowly open the door and hear Pastor Richards playing and singing his song.

~ If Only ~

There goes the alarm
It's time to start another day
But I'd rather not
I just wanna go my own way

I don't know what's wrong
I keep tripping over myself
But where can I go to keep from feeling overwhelmed

My failures are strong
I just can't seem to break away
Then I hear you say
Your mercies are new every day

Help me live like I'm free
Instead of dragging the chains
You've already broken from me
Help me walk day by day
Keep my eyes on the truth
My feet on the straight and narrow way
You've changed me from the man I used to be
So help me live, Lord, live like I'm free

Why am I so scared
I should just take you at your word
The line between faith and doubt is constantly blurred

I need to let go finally give it all I've got
Into your story, I should be a part of your plot

Help me live like I'm free
Instead of dragging the chains
You've already broken from me
Help me walk day by day
Keep my eyes on the truth
My feet on the straight and narrow way
You've changed me from the man I used to be
So help me live, Lord, live like I'm free

You've changed me from the man I used to be
So help me live, Lord, like I'm free

As the song ends, Renee claps, and Pastor Richards looks up. Pearl and Renee are walking down the aisle.

"I didn't know I had an audience," he says.

As they reach the stage, Pearl speaks up. "Sweetheart, we have news for you."

"All right, lay it on me, dear," he says.

"Renee and I have been going through Scripture, and she has just called out to God and been born again," Pearl says, rubbing Renee's back.

Renee, smiling, looks up at Pastor Richards.

Tears are now coming from his eyes as well. "Oh my, well, that is good news indeed."

23

You're Gonna What?

"Thanks for bringing me down here to pick it up, sis," Tony says as they walk the lot, heading for the front door.

"You're welcome, but are you sure about this? This is a big-ticket item. Shouldn't you talk to Mr. Ingles first and get some things set up before you spend this much money on a new car?" Renee asks, trying to reason with him as they walk through the door to the showroom.

"Done and done. I already have, sis. I just really want this, so I splurged just this once. I promise, this money is not going to ruin me. You'll see," Tony replies, trying to reassure Renee.

"Well, that's good news then."

I've got some more good news too."

"Mr. Edison, good to see you again. Come right this way," the salesman says, leading them to Tony's new purchase. "And is this the special lady you were telling me about?"

Renee smiles mischievously at Tony. "Do tell. Am I the special lady you told him about?"

At that, the salesman is a bit puzzled and has a look on his face that says he wishes he had not said that.

Tony shakes his head and then eases the salesman's mind. "This lady that is harassing me and making you feel uneasy is my special twin sister, and she is just messing around. I am heading over to pick up the other special lady when I leave here."

"Whew, all right then. I'm glad. I thought I put my foot in my mouth," he says as they turn the corner and Tony's car comes into view. "Well, here she is, Mr. Edison, your Audi R8, with its 4.2 liter V8 engine with 430 horsepower. She can go from 0 to 60 in 4.2 seconds, topping out at 176 miles per hour. She has the premium sound package. Well, you know. You ordered it special. All we need to do is get your John Hancock on this form taking receipt of the vehicle, and you're ready to go."

"She is some kinda beautiful," Tony says, walking around it, mesmerized. "What do you think, sis?"

"It definitely suits you. I love that deep blue color, and those headlights look so imposing."

"This will definitely be a spectacular setting for that proposal tonight," the salesman says as if he is continuing to sell the car.

"What!" Renee blurts out loudly, turning to Tony for confirmation, the entire dealership full of people now seemingly her audience. "You're gonna what?"

~ If Only ~

The salesman, realizing he has now let the cat, or possibly even Pandora, out of the proverbial box, backs up and tries to slip away to give them space to discuss this further.

Tony quickly steps closer to Renee and holds on to her shoulders. "Okay, maybe let's switch back to our indoor voice here, Renee."

"I'm sorry, but when were you gonna tell me this?"

"The plan was to get the car outside and then talk to you. Remember a few moments ago I said I had some more good news?" he says, quietly trying to put out the fire before it burns the whole place down.

"This is way too quick. I don't know what has gotten into you, but you just can't flip a switch and go from playboy to family man," Renee says in full sister-protecting-brother mode. "It's the money, isn't it? You told her about the money, and now she is pressuring you to get married." Now very animated and in attack position, she continues, "Well, she's just gonna have to sign a prenup. Yeah, that's it. There's no other way around it. I'll take care it. I'll call Mr. Ingles tomorrow. In fact, let me leave him a message right now," she exclaims as she starts thumbing the contacts list on her smartphone.

Tony reaches for her phone and pushes her hands down. "Renee, calm down. Here," he says, opening the car door. "Come sit down. Let's talk."

Renee walks around and sits in the car, and Tony shuts the door. As he walks around to the driver's seat, he smiles and nods to the other customers who are watching this scene unfold. Getting in the car himself, Tony puts an end to the drama, and everyone goes back to what they were doing.

"Renee, calm down. I haven't told Adrianna about the inheritance. All she knows is that my uncle died. I don't think I even mentioned his name. Trust me, she is not after any money," Tony says, trying his best to calm Renee down.

"Are you sure? I just don't want you to be taken advantage of. And why are you moving so fast anyway? This is not like you," she pleads.

"Look, you have had things on your mind lately, and so have I. It's time for me to leave the players' club lifestyle and commit to someone. You know, hearing about Uncle Lou and all he went through, I don't want to waste any more time. I want to be with the person that is right for me. This is not rash. It's not spur-of-the-moment. I really have put a lot of thought into this, and now that we can afford to do what we want with no financial burdens, I want to be with her. I love her."

"Wow. Okay," Renee concedes. "I waited a long time to hear you sound like this. I'm so happy for you," she says as her eyes well up, and she leans across the car to hug him. "Well, I hope things go the way you want and you have a great evening."

"Thanks, sis. So what are you and Jason doing tonight?

"We are planning on going to the movies," she replies.

"Don't forget to turn off your cell phone," he says, laughing a corny laugh.

"Yeah, I wouldn't want to disrupt things now, would I?"

24

A New Car?

Beep, beep, beep, beeep.

Adrianna looks out of her apartment window to see a car she doesn't recognize sitting at the curb. The driver, still behind the wheel, is steadily laying on the horn.

Beep, beep beeep.

She slips on her sneakers and runs out the door, waving her arms and shouting, "Cut it out, you idiot, or I'm calling the cops."

Just then, the passenger window lowers, and the man behind the wheel leans over. She is suddenly taken back by the thought that maybe running out alone to some maniac at the curb was not such a good idea, so she stops and backs up a couple of steps.

A familiar voice calls out to her. "Adrianna, sweetheart, it's me."

"Tony?" she answers, puzzled. "What are you doing? What is this? I thought we were going out to see a play tonight." She leans forward and bends down to see that it is really him.

"We are, we are, and we are going there in this." He turns off the engine and jumps out of the car with both hands raised and spread out. "Well, what do ya think?"

"It is very pretty, but what is it. Whose is it?" she asks nervously. "You didn't rent this just for tonight, did you?"

"This, my dear, is a childhood dream. I have always wanted a European sports car. Last month, we met with the lawyer, and we got the first draw of our inheritance from Uncle Lou. I went straight to the dealer and ordered this. They had this shipped in for me, and I picked it up at lunch today."

Overwhelmed by the whole thing, Adrianna slowly shakes her head and stutters just a bit as she says, "European sports car, huh? But you're too young for a midlife crisis. Isn't this waaay too expensive?"

"It's not a midlife crisis. I told you, it's a childhood dream. And, yes it is way too expensive, but this is the only splurging I did." As he says the words, he knows they are not the truth and reaches into his pocket to feel the small box hidden there. "Look, I don't want you to think that I am gonna go nuts and will be blowing money left and right. I promise you, I put the rest in the bank, and I have a meeting set up for Monday afternoon with a financial advisor."

"Wait a minute. European sports car, bank account, financial advisor? How much money are you talking about?"

she says with a look on her face that says she's not sure she's ready for the real answer.

"Um, well, I don't know yet for sure. You've heard of Hamilton Windows and Doors?"

She looks at him like she doesn't want to believe it but nods yes in response.

"Well, that was my Uncle Lou. He still owned 80 percent of the company when he died. My sister and I aren't the only ones named in the will. We have some cousins that are involved as well, but it will be a lot. We don't know all the details yet. We just got the first draw. I'm sorry, I guess I should've told you, but I didn't want it to affect how you felt about me."

"No, no. You're right. It's okay. You did the right thing. It's just a lot to take in," she says.

"Well, then don't. Just focus on tonight, and we'll leave the rest for another day," he replies, taking her hand and walking back toward her apartment.

"Okay. I can do that. So where are we eating anyway"

"I made reservations at Diner Aux Chandelles," he says, trying his best to sound French. "I hope you don't mind. I thought French fit the occasion." When Adrianna looked at him funny, he realized he was tipping his hand too much, so he quickly follows with, "You know, romantic dinner and then an off-Broadway play."

Adrianna's face relaxes as she nods and shrugs. "I guess that makes sense," she says.

~ If Only ~

Feeling like she bought it, he quickly leans in and kisses her, then pulls away. "Speaking of which, I guess we'd better get going," he says.

"Oh yeah. Give me just a few more minutes. I wasn't expecting you for another half hour," she says as she heads back to her bedroom. They continue to talk while she dresses and brushes her hair.

Anthony is sitting on her couch while she is getting ready. "Well, I was off work early, so I figured, why wait," he replies, grinning. "Plus I'm just excited about tonight. You know, I never have been to a play before." As he is talking, he reaches in his pocket and pulls out a small red box, which he opens to reveal a diamond ring. Looking at it, he smiles and then puts it away

"I've never seen a guy so excited to see a musical," Adrianna calls out to him. "I never would have thought I would be going to see a play either."

"War movies and stuff like that would normally be my style, but I'm really looking forward to it," Tony says.

"Me too," she replies. "I just think it's gonna be the perfect evening. You are really starting to surprise me."

"You ain't seen nothin' yet," he whispers to himself and grins.

"I won't be much longer," she says.

"Take your time. Everything's all right," he replies, pulling the ring out once again and smiling. Excited but nervous, he's hoping she won't turn him down, hoping that she won't think it's too soon. "At least I hope so."

"Why wouldn't it be?" Adrianna adds. "You and me, new car, French restaurant, and a musical—what could ruin that?"

"You're right. You're right, of course."

"As per usual." She giggles as the words slip out. "So what about Renee? What has she done with her money?" she asks.

"Well, you don't know Renee, but she is extremely cautious about everything. I'm sure by now her money is in a Swiss account being heavily guarded by an entire team," he says as he lets out a chuckle.

"I'm sure she's not that bad. Is she?"

"No, I'm just being facetious, but she has always been a bit skittish, never really likes to make a move on her own. She is so unsure of herself. I think she just feels better when she runs her decisions by someone, and usually it's me, which is okay. I like being her big brother, even if I'm only ten minutes older," he says, leaving out the fact that he talked his plans for the evening over with Renee.

"Almost done," Adrianna calls out

Tony, a little startled by the proclamation, drops the ring box to the floor and quickly scrambles to pick it up and put it back in his pocket. Just a little paranoid, he pulls it back out and checks it again to make sure it's still in the box and then puts it away.

Hearing her come out of the bedroom and shutting off the lights, Tony stands facing the hallway, awaiting her arrival. As she emerges out of the darkness, he is captivated by the sight of her, and all he can do is shake his head as she stands with her arms on her hips and a smile on her face.

"Okay, I'm ready. What's wrong?" she says.

"Not a thing. You're absolutely beautiful," he replies.

"You are so silly," she says as she grabs his elbow. "Let's get going."

25

Off We Go

Anthony pulls the door shut behind them and holds his elbow out for her again. Adrianna takes it and rests her head on his shoulder as they walk to the car. Holding the door for her, Anthony bows as he says, "My lady."

Willing to play along with him, she replies, "Thank you, kind sir," then giggles and gets into the car.

As they drive out of town, they continue the playful courting gestures, laughing at each other and themselves. Excited about the evening, Anthony is smiling more than even he thinks he is, which doesn't go unnoticed. Adrianna has been watching him, wondering, and can no longer hold it in.

"What are you up to tonight?" she says. "I've never seen you smiling so much. You're gonna make your face hurt." At that, she starts smiling herself.

Just as Anthony slows down for the entrance to the freeway, she reaches over and touches his face. He leans into it and closes his eyes for a brief second.

"I'm not up to anything," he replies. "I just love being with you."

Adrianna turns on the radio and finds some soft music for the rest of the trip. Listening to the music and watching as twilight comes on, Tony turns on the headlights along with many other drivers. His mind begins to drift to thoughts of his life and how it has all changed over the last few months. Thinking of all the dates and dancing, all the clubs and parties he's been to in his life, he begins to realize that for the first time in his life, he wants nothing more than someone to share life with, and he is sure that she is sitting next to him. The sun is gone now, and twilight prevails. Headlights and reflections dance across the windshield. Then suddenly, they see flashing blue lights up ahead. Traffic speeds slow down dramatically and then come to a stop. After a few moments, they move forward slowly, and Adrianna changes the radio to the traffic channel.

"There is a three-car pileup on the interstate tonight, and traffic is nearly stopped," the voice from the radio says.

"Sweetheart, can you see if you can figure out the GPS and find us an alternate road to take?" Tony asks.

"Oh yeah, sure, let me see," she replies and starts pushing buttons. "Ooh, ooh, what's that? No, no, no, go back. I really do hate these things," she says.

Tony smiles and moves the car forward a little.

"Okay, here we go," Adrianna says. "It looks like if we get off at the next exit, we can take a back road for a good ways and then get back on the freeway in about fifteen miles. How's that sound?"

"Perfect," Tony replies. "Thank you, sweetie."

Traffic moves very slowly for the next couple of miles, but they finally arrive at the exit, and, like many before them, they take it.

"Wow, look at the stars," Tony says. "You know, I hope the people in the accident are okay, but I'm glad for the detour. This is beautiful."

"I know. You're right. This is perfect," she replies.

Tony looks at the dashboard clock and thinks to himself, *We are okay time-wise, but we can't have any more delays.*

After a couple of miles, the road they are on clears out, and they can see no vehicles at all. Anthony looks at the road and then the stars and begins to think of how special even the drive is becoming. He looks over at Adrianna, thinking to himself how beautiful she is and how lucky he is. Adrianna glances over at him and smiles.

"You are so—" Tony begins to say but is quickly cut off.

"Tony, watch out!" she screams.

He turns his head back to see a deer standing in the middle of the road, straddling the line. He swerves to miss it, sending the passenger side tires off the pavement. Tony cuts the wheel back sharply, trying to get back on the road but overcompensates and causes the car to go into a roll. Everything seems to go in slow motion as the car rolls the first time, Adrianna's head hitting the passenger window, shattering it. Air bags go off, pushing both of them back into their seats, but the car keeps rolling, once, twice, three times.

Thaniel, just arriving to find them in danger, dives into the broken window to help cushion them from any further injury. His large wings keeping them pressed against their seats.

Finally the car comes to a stop on the fourth roll, landing on its roof. Crawling out of the car, Thaniel looks up and down the road and sees no vehicles in either direction. Panicking, he looks back at Tony and Adrianna and sees that she has blood streaming down her face and from her side. He tries to wake Anthony but to no avail. Standing up again, he sees that there is still no one coming.

26

Oh No

The sound of the car engine turning off wakes Anthony, but he is so disoriented he feels as if he is dreaming. Nothing is making sense. He can hear a cell phone being dialed, then the ringing sound as a call is being placed.

"911, what is your emergency?" says the voice on the other in of the call.

A haggard voice replies, "My name is Anthony Edison. I've been in a crash. I'm on Route 5 about thirty miles outside the city. My car is upside down, and my girlfriend won't wake up."

The voice sounds very similar to his own, but he doesn't recognize it. Why would someone be making a call in his name? Was it someone else or himself? Everything seems so foggy. He can't keep his eyes open and finally gives up and dozes off again.

~ If Only ~

Anthony tries to open his eyes to see what all the noises around him are, but he is very tired, and his head is throbbing. He can sense the flurry of activity going on. Sounds fill the air—sirens, people screaming, vehicle after vehicle coming closer. Then he suddenly remembers the crash, the feeling of helplessness as the car tumbled over and over before finally coming to an upside-down stop. He recognizes the faint hissing sound of the spewing radiator. With heart-pounding terror, he finally realizes that Adrianna had been in the crash with him and looks over to see if she is all right. She is breathing but unresponsive as medics reach the car and begin feverishly working to get her out of it. One of them notices his open eyes and motions to another arriving team of medics to go to his side of the vehicle. Suddenly before him are two feet, then two knees, then two hands, and then a woman's face tilted sideways, looking at him.

"Are you okay, sir? Can you tell me your name?" she says.

Frantically he replies, "Is she okay? Adrianna? Is she gonna be okay?"

The medic looks across the inside of the vehicle to the others who are helping Adrianna. One of them looks back at her with a shrug and mouths the words, "I don't know." Looking back at Tony, she says, "You know what, Adrianna has some really good people helping her. I promise I will keep an eye on her as much as I can, but right now, I need to focus on you. My name is Kathryn. Can you tell me your name?"

Tired and frustrated, he looks over at Adrianna and lets out a deep sigh, realizing there is nothing he can do for her. He relaxes and lets gravity pull him downward into his seat belt. Turning back to look at Kathryn, he says, "Anthony. My name is Anthony or Tony. Either is okay."

"Anthony, huh? Okay, yeah, I can see you as an Anthony. Now, Anthony, I need you to tell me how you are doing because I can't see blood or anything. So what are you feeling right now?" she replies, glad to see that he is responding.

Overwhelmed by everything, he thinks for a moment longer than she would prefer, so she asks again, "Anthony, how are you feeling?"

He blinks quickly as he focuses on Kathryn and says, "I'm…I'm okay. I just have a headache, a throbbing headache."

Kathryn smiles and says, "Thank you, Anthony. Now we are gonna put a brace on your neck and slowly pull you out of the vehicle, okay?"

He slowly replies, "Okay." Hearing activity on the other side, he turns to see Adrianna being pulled free from the car.

"Stay with me now, handsome." She waves her hand before his eyes, drawing them back to her. "So tell me, Tony, what happened here? How did you guys end up like this?"

"Um," Tony replies, groggy but trying to remember. "Deer. It was a deer. It was standing in the road. I didn't see it soon enough. I was looking at Adrianna."

"Well, she is a looker now, isn't she?" Kathryn says, thankful Tony is engaged still in the conversation. Lying on her back, she scoots her way into position and reaches up to put the brace around Tony's neck. Rolling away and back to her knees, she says, "All right now, sweetie, my partner Steve is gonna use a pry bar to get your door open, so it's probably gonna be loud."

Before he has a chance to reply, the sound of a landing helicopter takes everyone's attention. Looking out the windshield, Tony watches as the medics push Adrianna's gurney out toward it. The screeching sound of the crunching car door pulls Tony's focus back to Kathryn and Steve, who are now both on their knees pulling a gurney for him into place.

Steve grabs a long spine board and slides it beneath Tony, and both medics prepare to move him.

"Okay, buddy, are you ready?" Steve asks.

Tony, now weary of looking at everyone upside down, answers with a sigh and a nod.

"He we go," Kathryn says as she pushes the button on Tony's seat belt. As the pressure releases him, Steve pulls him toward the board, and Kathryn helps move him into place. With straps holding him in place, they lift him up and onto the gurney.

As he is being rolled toward the ambulance that is to carry him to the hospital, he sees the helicopter that is carrying Adrianna taking off.

"Where are they taking her?" he asks fearfully.

Kathryn, reaching for his hand, replies, "You're following right behind her. We just need to get her there faster okay. You'll see her soon."

"Kathryn," Steve calls out, motioning to get her attention.

She looks up to see him holding a white feather in his hand. "What's this?" she replies.

"I dunno," he says, shrugging his shoulders with both eyes wide open. "But I thought Tony said he saw a deer."

27

In the Chapel

"Mr. Edison, you're all set to go. Now make sure you call your local emergency room or your doctor if you have any other issue all right?" a nurse says to Tony as she hands him his release papers.

"Where can I go to find out about my girlfriend?" Tony asks, visibly shaken.

The nurse, looking at him, sympathetically responds, "I really don't think they are going to tell you anything. Isn't there anyone of her family members here to help you?"

"No, no one is here yet. Please?"

Sighing, she tells him, "Go to the nurses' desk on the third floor. I don't think they will tell you anything, but you can try. The elevator is down this hall to the right." She points in the direction he needs to go.

"Sir, all I will tell you is that she is still in surgery, and I'm really not supposed to tell you that. I really am sorry, but

I'm not allowed to share any information with anyone but family," the third-floor nurse says as calmly as she can.

"I'm not trying to be difficult," Tony says, then starts fumbling through his pockets. Pulling out the little jewelry store box, he opens it to show its contents to the nurse. "I was going to propose tonight," he says, looking down at the diamond ring, "but then we had the crash, and everything is upside down."

"Oh man, you're gonna get me fired. Look, I can't tell you anything, but I'll find some sort of way to let you know something. Please, though, go somewhere and try to relax—the waiting room or the chapel but not here. I'll find you when I know something," the nurse, looking around, nervously, begs.

The waiting room was full, and Tony couldn't stand all the noise, so he headed down the hall toward the chapel. The walk seemed to take years. The sounds from every room torment him, making him think so many horrible thoughts, making every fear rise to the surface all at once.

Finally reaching the door, he slowly opens it, hoping for an empty room. Halfway to the front, however, is a lone figure—Thaniel, quietly sitting. Tony hesitantly walks to the front. Tears streaming down his face, he falls down to his knees at the altar. He quietly sobs at first, but it doesn't take long for a full cry to escape him. Soon the carpet is soaked, and his wails echo off the walls. Thaniel lays a hand on Tony's shoulder.

"Can I pray with you, friend?" he softly speaks.

Tony looks over his shoulder enough to reply, "I'm sure you have your own troubles."

"We all have troubles, but just for a few moments, let's just say that your troubles are my troubles," Thaniel offers back.

Tony stands up, and Thaniel motions for him to have a seat. Tony pulls out his ring once again and shows Thaniel.

"I see," Thaniel says at the sight of it. "I take it things have not turned out quite the way you imagined tonight?"

"I was looking at her while I was driving. Then a deer was just there. I swerved too much, and when I cut the wheel back, the car started flipping. Now here we are, with her in surgery." Tony's whole body slouches in exhaustion.

"I'm so sorry," Thaniel says. "What about you? Are you all right?"

"I'm fine, just going out of my mind," Tony replies, wiping his eyes again. "I just keep thinking, praying for God to help. I told Him I would do anything He wanted if He would just let her pull through this."

"I don't think it really works like that," Thaniel says.

"What?" Tony looks over at him, puzzled.

Thaniel sits up straight. "Well, I mean, are you doing what He wants you to do now? Are you living for Him now?"

Tony sighs. "Why should he do anything for me, right? I guess I have been living a pretty horrible life—drinking too much, girl after girl. I feel different about Adrianna, though."

"How about God? Do you feel any different about Him?"

Tony sits for a moment and thinks.

"God simply wants us. He wants us to love Him and live a holy life for Him. Will He give us everything we ask for if we do? No, but He will help us through whatever we face if we love Him and trust Him," Thaniel reasons.

"What do I do?" Tony asks.

"We can't put God in a box, my friend," Thaniel replies. "You need to give God your heart. Ask for His son, Jesus, to be your Savior and tell Him you'll live for Him now, regardless of the outcome of Adrianna's surgery."

Tony, crying again, says, "I know, I know. I'm just so scared."

"In Job 13:15, Job says of God, 'Though he slay me yet will I trust him.' Step out and trust him like that, and He will help you," Thaniel pleads with Tony.

Tony looks up at Thaniel. "Okay, I will. Will you pray with me?"

"I would like nothing better than to pray with you, Tony," Thaniel says, finally smiling.

28

Please Wake Up

Pastor and Mrs. Richards arrive at the hospital. They quickly make their way to the emergency room desk.

"Hello, how can I help you tonight?" the voice behind the glass says.

"Hi, we are looking for Adrianna Portal and Anthony Edison," Pastor Richards says, both him and his wife swaying nervously back and forth.

"Which one are you family of?" the voice asks.

"Neither," Pearl answers.

"I'm their pastor," David adds.

"Oh well, Anthony Edison has been released. As for Adrianna Portal, give me a moment to talk to my supervisor please," the lady says and then walks across the room. Reaching a woman at another desk some fifty feet away, she begins to talk.

Pearl and David both furl their eyebrows and look at each other, shrugging as well. Looking back to the two women, they see the one behind the counter is pointing in their direction and talking very fast, though they can't hear anything. Another couple walks up in line behind and asks where the person is that is supposed to be behind the desk. They both turn to look and see who it is and at the same time point in the direction of the two women talking in private. The two couples watch intently as the two ladies break their huddle and start approaching. The first lady resumes her post behind the desk as her supervisor comes around to talk to David and Pearl.

"So you two are asking to see Adrianna Portal?"

"Yes," all four bystanders answer, and then everyone begins looking puzzled. The couple who just arrived says, "How did you know?"

The supervisor, now very confused, answers, "I was speaking to them, but you want to see her as well?"

"We're her parents."

"Well then, who are you?" the supervisor directs her question to David and Pearl.

"I'm her pastor, and this is my wife," David replies.

"Oh," Adrianna's parents and the supervisor say in unison, as if a lightbulb went on.

"Well, now that her parents are here as well, this is much easier," the supervisor says. "Do you mind if they hear?"

"Of course not. Hear what? Is she all right?" Adrianna's father responds. "Where is Tony?"

"I'm not sure exactly where Tony is. I haven't seen him since he was released. Adrianna is still in surgery. There is a waiting room on the third floor where you'll be closer to her if you like."

Reaching the third floor, the group checks in at the nurses' station.

"I'm so glad that you all have made it. Tony was so upset I couldn't give him any updates, but now that you are here…," the nurse says, looking at Adrianna's parents. "She suffered a ruptured spleen and has a lot of internal bleeding, as well as cuts and bruises. She is still in surgery, but if you'd like to sit in the waiting room, I will update you again as soon as I know something new."

Sitting down in the waiting room, David turns to Pearl. "I think I'm going to see if I can find Tony. Are you okay sitting with Adrianna's parents?"

"Of course, darling, go."

Finally making his way to the chapel, David slowly opens the door to see Tony on his knees at the altar. His eyes welling up at the sight he has longed to see for so long, he slowly walks the aisle. Kneeling close, David rests an arm across Tony's shoulders. Flinching slightly, Tony finishes his prayer and then opens his eyes and turns to see his new company.

"Pastor, thank you for coming," Tony says.

"Of course, I'm so glad you called me," he replies.

"I called you?" Tony asks, searching his mind but unable to recall doing so. "I don't even remember doing it. Wait a minute." Tony stops and looks around the room. "Where's that guy? There was a guy in here talking to me."

Tony and David stand to look the room over but find no one.

"I don't see anyone, Tony. Are you sure you're all right?" David says, resting a hand on his shoulder again.

"Pastor," Tony says, bewildered and still looking around, "there was a man here talking and praying with me. I asked Jesus to save me. Then while I was praying, you appeared and touched me."

"Wow. Tony, you are giving me chills. I'm so happy to hear that."

"Do you think…do you think I was talking with an angel?" Tony asks suspiciously, unsure if he should ask.

"I can't say, but maybe it's better not knowing for sure, don't you think?" David responds. "Come on, let's go sit with Adrianna's parents."

"They're here?" Tony asks.

"Yes, and your sister is on the way. They said you called her too."

Tony closes his eyes and holds his head. "I don't remember any of that. Maybe I should sit down."

As Tony and David make it back to the waiting room, the third-floor nurse comes running.

"There you are. Come with me. She's out of surgery and in a room now," the nurse says, smiling but out of breath from the running.

"Oh my gosh, so she's okay?" Tony asks.

"Come see for yourself," the nurse says.

Knocking twice quickly on the door to Adrianna's room, the nurse slowly opens it and peeks in. Smiling, she turns back to Tony and David and then opens the door, letting them in.

Nervously walking in, Tony eyes drip tears once again as he sees Adrianna. When she sees him, she says in a groggy voice, "I thought I lost you."

Tony, weeping, replies, "I thought I lost you."

An hour or so passes, and everyone has settled down from all the excitement, everyone but Tony. His hand in his pocket most of the time, he could think of nothing except the plans that had been ruined by the car crash. He was just about to speak when there was a knock on the door. Pastor Richards, being the closest, reaches for the handle and slowly opens it. Renee and Jason walk in, glad to see that Tony and Adrianna are both safe and secure. Running over to Tony, Renee hugs him first.

"I'm glad you are okay," she says and then goes to the bed to greet Adrianna.

"Me too," Tony replies. "I'm glad you two made it here safely."

Hugging Adrianna, Renee says, "How are you doing? In a lot of pain?"

"Not too bad right now, but I'm sure it will hit me later," Adrianna replies, wincing slightly at the pressure from the hug.

"I still don't know how you had wits enough about you to call me," Renee says, looking back at Tony.

"I don't know. Apparently I made a lot of calls, but I don't remember any of it," he says, shaking his head.

"It's okay, Tony, don't worry yourself about that stuff," Renee says and comes back to sit by him.

Tony stands and, unable to wait any longer, speaks up. "Since everyone is here and Adrianna is doing better, there is something I would like to say."

Everyone turns to look at him.

Tony steps in close and takes Adrianna's hand. "I had this special evening planned that obviously did not include any of this, but all of this reaffirms my plans for tonight. I have been so afraid I was gonna lose you for the last couple of hours."

Looking around at everyone, he continues, "We were headed to see a play tonight when the crash occurred. I had made arrangements with the theater for Adrianna and I to come up onto the stage at intermission."

Adrianna's eyebrows furrow, wondering why and what was to come.

Finally, he pulls the little box he has been very anxiously waiting to show her all day out of his pocket and opens it for her to see.

"Sweetheart," he says, his eyes welling up again, "will you marry me?"

Epilogue

Two and a half years later

The sun shines brightly on a beautiful spring morning. Flowers and trees are in full bloom, and the world is alive and abuzz again. The church parking lot begins to fill. Everyone is cheerful and bouncy as they make their way into the building. The auditorium is adorned with hundreds of wonderfully fragrant flowers, and beautiful ribbons and bows are draped everywhere. The piano is being softly played so as to provide ambiance but not to drown out the chatter of the crowd. Tony is walking with purpose as he crosses the vestibule area and walks down the hallway toward the pastor's office, lights, as usual, coming on just before he needs them. His face is all aglow, his eyes bright and wide open. Stopping at Mrs. Richards's office door, he softly knocks. Cracking the door open, Tony peeks in and then enters.

"Oh, Tony, you look so good in that tux," Renee says. "You can't make me cry today. Not yet."

"What about you? You're beautiful. Everything is perfect, sis," Tony says, looking at Renee in her wedding gown.

He moves in for a quick hug.

"Okay, not too much. You can hug me later."

"All right, all right. I'm not gonna mess you up," he says.

"I wish Mom and Dad could be here," Renee says, fighting back the tears.

"I know. That's all I've thought about today," Tony says, taking a step back from her.

"Do you think they can see from up there?" Renee asks, looking toward the sky.

Shrugging his shoulders, Tony answers, "I don't know, but I'd like to think so."

"Oh yeah," Tony says, eyes wide open like a child. "Jason is here, and so far I haven't seen any pregnant screaming girlfriends running around."

"That's enough, Anthony," she says, laughing and smacking his shoulders.

"Aaah, you know I'm just kidding."

"I know, and thank you…for confirming both of those things for me," Renee replies smiling.

"Okay, well, I'd better go sit down. Congratulations, sis. I love you," Tony says.

"Okay, I love you too," Renee replies.

Tony leaves, shutting the door behind him. Renee steps back in front of the mirror and looks herself over one last time. Then checking the clock, she picks up her bouquet and waits for Tony to come back.

~ If Only ~

"It's me again," he says as he comes through the door.

"You forgot you are giving me away?" she asks, smiling.

"Of course not. Just wanted you to think that," he says, holding out his arm.

Thaniel sits quietly in the back row of the church. His joy is not just for the ceremony to come but for finally being able to see not just one but two come to the Lord. Excitement bubbling over inside of him, he decides to text his friends.

> Haniel, where are you two?

Really, again with the texting?

> Yep, I'm happy. It's a good day.

Yes, it is, and you have had quite a few good days lately.

> I have. Thank you both for your help.

You're welcome.

> Is Jankiel with you?

Yes, we are headed your way.

> I will see you shortly then.

All right.

The groomsmen and the bridesmaids are all in position, and the flower girl has laid flower petals to mark the path. The music ends, and a hush fills the auditorium.

The wedding march begins, and the entire congregation stands to honor the bride. Renee and Tony appear in the doorway and begin the slow journey to the altar, where Jason is waiting. As the twins enter the doorway, Tony looks down for just a split second, and his eyes focus on a single white feather under the last row of seats. As he ponders the find, he thinks to himself, *That's odd*. Renee pulls his attention back to the moment.

"Isn't this all beautiful?" Renee says, leaning close to Tony.

"Yes, it is, and it's all for you, sis. You deserve this, so enjoy it," he answers.

Starting to get choked up, she responds only by squeezing his arm.

Reaching the first row of guests and the end of the song, Renee and Tony stop and wait for Pastor Richards, who is at the pulpit awaiting his turn.

"Dearly beloved, we are gathered here today to join in holy matrimony Renee Edison and Jason Westwood. Who gives the bride?" David proclaims.

"I do," Tony answers as he releases her so she could step forward and join hands with Jason.

Tony looks to the seat where Adrianna sits holding their baby girl. She smiles at him, and he smiles back.

"It is the bride's wish that before we continue any further, we offer this one opportunity for anyone who may object or show just cause why these two should not be joined. Let them speak now or forever hold their peace."

Tony turns to sit down beside Adrianna, and as he does, he sees a man standing against the back wall. Thaniel, standing alone, makes eye contact with Tony and nods. Tony nods back and sits. During the moment of silence, Tony recognizes the face as Thaniel's and quickly stands and turns to see him again. When he looks, there is no one there.

"What's wrong?" Adrianna asks.

Tony sits, a puzzled look on his face. Suddenly his mind flashes back to the night two and a half years earlier, the night he proposed to Adrianna, the night that had so many highs and lows—a brand-new dream car, a perfectly planned evening, a diamond ring, a beautiful woman, the deer that he saw too late, the crash and the paramedics, the trembling and crying and praying in the hospital chapel, and the mysterious figure that talked and reasoned and prayed with him. Last of all, he thinks of the lonely feather he saw lying on the floor under the last row as he walked his sister down the aisle. Tony looks back one more time just to be sure of who he saw.

Adrianna, now a bit unnerved, asks again, "Sweetheart, what is wrong?"

Then shaking his head, he looks at her and smiles as he says, "Nothing, not a thing."

Companion Section

Music and poetry are very dear to my heart. I believe there is a certain romance inside us all for the things that we love, whether it be our family, a pet, a car, or a particular event. I thought it would be fascinating to look inside some of the character's thoughts during their lives through poems. Each poem will correlate to a particular section of the story. I hope you find it helpful.

Thaniel

Thaniel wrote these two poems at the thought the years of life that passed by as he continued to care for Louis:

Sands

The sun rises as brilliantly today as it did yesterday.
The wind keeps blowing mysteriously by.
The sands continue to fall.

A spark ignites a flame that burns hotter than a summer day
As a storybook sky hangs over our heads.

The sands continue to fall.

Affectionate seeds sprout into new life
And soon yield their bountiful harvest.
The sands continue to fall.

The face of the moon changes faithfully. Aged stars rocket across
The black violet canvas and then burn out.
The sands continue to fall.

Disagreeing storms devour and quench the sultry blaze leaving
The embers smoldering in their own suffocating smoke.
The sands continue to fall.

Hunger turns into despair so close to apathy
That it is almost impossible to tell the difference.
The sands continue to fall.

Tomorrow the sun will rise, the winds will blow, sparks will ignite,
Seeds will sprout, the moon will change, stars will die,
Clouds will storm, embers will smolder.
The sands will continue to fall.

How Long?

A voice from eternity cries out…

How long shall my arms stay open…empty?

~ If Only ~

How long shall they continue to reach out,
  my hands grasping and pulling back only air?

How long shall your tender face be turned,
  hidden from eyes?

How long shall my ears be deafened by
  your unwavering silence?

How long shall I be patient,
  my emotions and desires
    left dry and unquenched?

How long, dear soul,
  how much longer shall I wait
  for you to come to Calvary's cross?

Thaniel wrote this poem as he watched Renee's heart changing, getting closer to God:

It Is Time

It is time, darling sparrow.
Dive from your nest, into the sky.
I know your heart is racing and the tree is tall,
But until you do, you cannot fly.

It is time, spotted fawn.
Stand and bask in the morning sun.
I know your legs wobble and the grass is wet,
But until you do, you cannot run.

It is time, my little hero.
Take a breath and swing your bat.
I know that you are nervous for the pitcher throws
   so hard.
But until you do, you will not get a hit.

It is time, my young apprentice.
Guide your brush with all your heart.
Transform you blank white canvas and let the world
behold the splendor of your classic art.

This poem was written by Thaniel after Tony proposed to Adrianna.

What Color?

What color will you turn
In the autumn of your life?
When bitter winds blow
Bringing heartache and strife.

Will you be a dazzling red
When you're persecuted by the world?
How about a fiery orange as
Satan's darts at you are hurled?

Will you beam a brilliant yellow
Going on to meet the Lord without a frown?
Hold to your faith in Jesus
E'er your trials turn you brown.

Keep your sword, the Word of God, ever by your side.
Send your prayers forth night and day.
May the blessed Holy Spirit be your guide
And the Lord give grace to help you on your way.

Renee

Renee wrote "Grip" and "The Face" in the weeks following Louis's funeral as she struggled with the thoughts of her own mortality.

Grip

My spirit, the energy deep within me that creates the visible signs of who I really am, is trembling. It has for been some time now, as if in the presence of some great and awful terror, yet without that terror ever knowing that I exist and without me ever realizing what the terror really is.

Why, why do I quiver? Because I am uncertain of myself, or maybe that I am afraid of the future? I am not certain, for nothing has recently changed that should cause me such great discomfort. If I was not worried before, I should be fine. If I was anxious before, why am I only now shaken?

I am now so stirred—to the point of utter disgust. My thoughts are consumed only by what will put an end to this petrifying apprehension. Things in my life that should bring me great joy only moderately please me. I will certainly be relieved when this overly persistent grip is loosed, and I may breathe effortlessly once again. It would feel so good to finally be free from this pain.

The Face

As darkness draws my eyelids closed, my mind begins to drift. I find myself in an all too familiar place. Driving on a dangerous road filled with curves and hills, I notice that I am being followed. An obscure spectral figure appears in my mirrors, overwhelming me.

My instincts take over. My foot presses harder on the accelerator, but there is no escaping my pursuer. Together we travel in and out of the midmorning fog. Yet with every glance I take, I still cannot clearly make out who or what it is that gives me such a relentless chase.

Every turn only diminishes the distance between us, and my heartbeat quickens almost to a breaking point. Twisting and turning, my mind is now frantic, with no deliverance in sight. I can no longer tell if I am running away from or toward my stalker. I slam on my brakes and come to a squealing, spinning stop, leaving marks in the middle of the road!

~ If Only ~

As my headlights peer into the thick gray, my eyes begin to focus on the shadowy shape before me. It is the face of my pain.

Renee wrote these two poems after having accepted Jesus as her Savior:

I Will Sail On

I stand on the shore looking out
at the wind-tossed waves.
I should feel safe and secure…but I don't.
I am only here for a brief respite
and then I must go back out
to face the water's wrath again.

Somehow my tiny vessel has survived
the violent thrashing of the angry sea
but I must soon suffer it to transport me
once more.

This heavy, salt-soaked air
is suffocating me. The dark sky is filled
with menacing storm clouds
striking fear deep into my heart
until every bone aches and trembles.

But I will sail on,
for off in the far corner of the distant horizon
I can faintly see
a shimmer of golden sunlight…
and I will set my course for it.

Free

I needed a vacation, but it was hard for me to choose.
After much deliberation, I decided on an ocean cruise.

While lounging on the upper deck,
I saw a woman leaning on the rail.
Smiling with her arms spread open wide,
she breathed in the ocean air as if to be a human sail.
I asked her what she could be thinking,
that could fill her heart with such glee.
She replied that it was, "Nothing really,
it just somehow makes me feel free."

I watched from my front porch
a boy standing in the evening breeze.
With his arms spread wide open, he smiled,
as the air set his spirit at ease.
That simple act made him content,
as though his heart had not a plea.
When I questioned why, he said,
"This just makes me feel free."

In my sleep last night, I saw a vision
of the crucifixion of my Lord.
His arms were spread wide open,
as they raised that rugged cross.
I saw the Father turn His back on Him.
And I heard Him as He cried.
Yet through it all, he was still smiling,

So I asked Him just before He died,
"Lord, how can it be that you are happy
through all your pain and misery?"
"Because," He said, "my child, it is finished.
I have finally made you free."

Louis

Louis wrote "When, She" shortly after marrying Virginia.

When, She

When I am drawn outdoors by the warm summer sun,
She takes my hand and walks with me.
When I fail to hide my faults,
She still sees the man I want to be.
When the moon rises and darkness falls all around us,
She holds me close in sleepy bliss.
When my heart is troubled by visions in the night,
She calms me with her velvet kiss.

When she wants to light my fire,
She sparks me with her captivating glare.
When the weight of the world is too heavy for me,
She reminds me she is there.

When I'm worn down by a virus,
She stays home to comfort me.
When I talk about the future,
She shares in all my dreams.

When I have something on my mind,
She listens carefully to each verse.
When I ask if she will love me all my life,
She says no, she will love me all of hers.

With a broken heart that would never mend, Louis wrote these poems in the years following Virginia's death.

Good-bye

I can't believe you said good-bye.
I leave you dejected. My heart is crumbling,
falling to new depths within me.
I start my car, although only out of habit and necessity.
I am thankful for the highway's painted lines.
They, at least, give me some direction.
For without you, I don't know which way
I am supposed to go.

My eyes are drowning in a well of tears,
which refuse to stream down my face.
It's amazing there are any left at all.

My hands are trembling, frantically,
for I am in withdrawal…from you.
My whole being is craving you uncontrollably.
Everything I drive past reminds me of you,
torturing me that much more,
making my heart ache ever so excruciatingly.

Suddenly, I see the morning sun break through
our bedroom window. I turn over and
you are there, sleeping peacefully.
With a sigh of relief, I gently kiss your forehead
and go back to sleep.

Without You

Without you…
My days can't hope to be right.
No matter how good they are,
I'm still alone throughout the night.

Without you…
I can't bring myself to smile.
And every time I do,
It only lasts a short while.

Without you…
I can't find my way around.
And no matter how high I fly,
I come crashing to the ground.

Without you…
My life just won't be complete.
It sounds so empty inside,
With one lonely heartbeat.

Without you…
For me there's no happiness.
Will I ever find it again?
Well, now that's anyone's guess.

Flame

I remember many days gone by.
When I journeyed through the wilderness
on dark and stormy nights. I was not afraid
because I kept you, my lovely candle, close to me.
Burning so bright, your soft golden glow
lit my path and warmed my heart. Your sweet scent
soothed my soul. Though the world around me
may turn upside down, when I gazed at your flame,
all was well. Your light was my substance and my shield.
But now you fire has gone out.
It has drowned in its own waxy pool
of melted passion. Lonely winds are whistling
all around, freezing my soul, and my heart
grows numb from the pain. I am left
in darkness with no path to follow.

Wound

Once again thoughts of you have slashed my heart.
Though they come as no surprise,
they still cause tears to bleed from my eyes.

I keep myself as busy as I can,
but it's like a bandage that only hides
the cut that has destroyed my life.

The golden rays at daybreak
gently lull my pain to sleep.
But the dark of night reminds me that the gash is deep.

All I have to do is think of you,
and the hurt grabs me once again.
There is no place inside that it hasn't been.

Dreams quickly turn to nightmares
when my fate they seal
by foretelling that this awful wound will never heal.

Tony

Tony wrote these two poems in the days after watching Adrianna drive from the church parking lot without speaking to him.

Anticipation

Anticipation
> completely bittersweet expectation.

So sweet
> with its seducing promise of reward.

Yet so bitter
> in its icy relenting patience.

Every prize and longing
> dangling before me, just out of reach…
> I am forced into composure.

Being accustomed to
> accomplishments by my own hands…
> I grow increasingly restless.

Believing that time
> is one price…
> I can ill-afford to pay.

Yet
> the majestic beauty of the Blue Ridge Mountains,
> the overwhelming splendor of the Grand Canyons,
> the imposing charm of the Redwood Forest…
> all were perfected over many generations.

So
> I must learn patience,
> patience to let the water boil,
> patience to give the bread time to rise,
> patience to allow life to live.

Wait

You gotta wait
Yeah, they say you gotta wait
'cause the best things in your life
don't just happen every day.

And I've learned that some things
really are worth waiting for.

So until you tell me
you don't feel the same way too,
I'll hold on 'cause
I don't know what else to do.

This one he wrote after they patched things up:

Sunrise

Sunrise is so much sweeter
after the struggle of the storm.

Like my darling's arms,
it reaches through the clouds to keep me warm.

Hushing the thunder's angry words,
it makes my morning calm.

It breaks the lonely, separating darkness,
restoring joy to my soul.

Like a tender, reconciling kiss,
it brings comfort to my heart.

It is her reassuring smile
saying…I love you.

Tony wrote these three poems during the months of his courtship to Adrianna:

Whispering Cascade

Her voice, such a tender delicate timbre,
every word spoken more glorious
than the one before.

Like a warm summer breeze
flowing gently through a million pine trees,
kissing every needle along the way.

When she speaks my name, I become that forest,
swaying back and forth as I consume every drop
of her satin sonance, which echoes inside my mind.

I am entranced by the sight of her
velvet lips, as the notes roll
effortlessly from them,
like a trickling country stream.
I sit on the riverbank, dipping gently
into her engaging whispering cascade.

When my heart is heavy,
I close my eyes and lie back in her arms,
drifting away on her tranquil tones
until peace is restored to my soul.

Interlude

In a million unfamiliar faces,
there is no solitude,
and so my thoughts drift back to traces
of her, which keeps my soul subdued.
My arms, craving her embraces,
have lost their fortitude.

Back and forth a thousand paces,
my legs in loyal servitude march
as each forlorn foot traces
its lonely habitude.

Now my heart down deep within races
as I hear her sweet prelude,
and quickly all my pain erases
while we share an interlude.

Vacation

A time to pull away from the burdens of life.
A time to get away from the toils of the day.
A time to drive away from responsibilities
for just a short while.

A trip to breathe freely the exhilarating mountain air
and enjoy the wondrous view,
knowing that a new day is dawning.

A trip to feel the caresses of
soft soothing sands and silky ocean waves
while warm sun rays soak into your skin,
relaxing you thoroughly.

A trip to see the sparkling city lights
and behold the limitless possibilities before you,
regretting only that there is not enough time
to experience them all.

Others may need these trips.
I do not.
All these blessings come to me
every time I am alone with you.

Tony wrote this poem for Adrianna for their first anniversary.

Every Kiss

In days gone by, great storm clouds came,
bringing cold and heavy rains,
flooding, pouring over my heart,
driving happiness away.

Then suddenly, heaven's mercy
sent a flower from the sun
to warm my soul with soft embrace
'til the twain had become one.

You turned my wrong into a song.
My life with joy does burst
With a playful glance, a gentle touch,
and every kiss is as the first.

Pastor Richards

Pastor Richards wrote this for Pearl:

Until All Your Tears Are Gone

You've always done things by yourself.
It's not in you to ask for help.
Though sometimes I wish you would.
I want to be there by your side,
to hold you when you need to cry.
In bad times and in good,

~ If Only ~

I've tried so hard to let it show,
but it seems my love's misunderstood,
it seems you still don't know.

Everyone can use a helping hand,
someone who will understand
and be there to the end.
Don't be afraid to reach out for me
'cause one thing I can guarantee.
In me you can depend.

I know it sounds too good to be true,
someone to take care of you,
but if you marry me,
I'll be here for you when your heart's about to break.
I'll be here while you are sleeping and when you
   awake.
I won't tell you what to do, just help you see your
   troubles through. When you feel you can't go on,
   I'll hold you
until all your tears are gone.

These four are songs Pastor Richards wrote and sang at church.

In the Midst of the Thorns

Many years ago in a faraway land,
Father Abraham took his son by the hand.
He led him straight to the top of the hill,
where he bound him up, a sacrifice to kill.

When the Lord saw his faith clearly on display,
He sent His angel down to make another way.

And there all alone in the midst of the thorns
stood the lamb of God waiting to be torn.
With no fault of his own, yet condemned to die.
Though he could've escaped, he didn't even try.
To do the Lord's will is why he was born.
So he just stood there still in the midst of the thorns.

Away in a manger on that silent night,
God's holy child was born, full of truth and light.
The hungry He fed, the sick He did heal,
but the world , they mocked, and the world, they reeled.
He came to seek and to save that which was lost
and to give Himself as redemption's cost.

And there all alone in the midst of the thorns
stood the Lamb of God waiting to be torn.
With no fault of his own, yet condemned to die.
Though He could've escaped, He didn't even try.
To do the Lord's will is why He was born.
So He just stood there still in the midst of the thorns.

Here He Come (The Victory Song)

As I read God's Word tonight, all about the resurrection day, how we in Christ shall be caught up to go that heavenly way, my heart was so stirred inside, my eyes could not restrain tears of joy at the thought that Jesus Christ will come again. Then I began to imagine just what it will be like and what we will be thinking when we take that heavenly flight.

Here He comes, for to meet us in the air.
Yes, the trumpet's finally blown
and I can see Him standing there.
Here we go, with Him to be forevermore.
Rising high into the clouds
with our voices singing loud,
here He comes.

What a morning that will be.
Friends and loved ones we will see
and many that we never met before.
The Son of God will be our reigning King eternally
and we'll live forever on that peaceful shore.

Here He comes, for to meet us in the air.
Yes, the trumpet's finally blown
and I can see Him standing there.
Here we go, with Him to be forevermore.
Rising high into the clouds
with our voices singing loud,
here He comes.

Have You Considered the Saviour Today?

Every good and perfect gift comes down from above
from the Father of lights, with unsearchable love.
To each, something different, some diamonds, some
    pearls.

What a shame it would be not to share with the world.
> Have you considered the Saviour today?
> Have you thanked Him for blessings He's laid in your way?
> Have you asked for His guidance that you need not stray?
> Have you considered the Saviour today?

When this life has you troubled and great are your cares, remember sweet Jesus will always be there.
When you see that your brother has burdens like you, kneel with him in prayer and together get through.
> Have you considered the Saviour today?
> When your storm overwhelms you, don't turn away.
> He has power and riches, all you need do is pray.
> Have you considered the Saviour today?

Dear soul, are you trying to reach Heaven alone?
Good works will never be enough on their own.
You must trust in Jesus, who died for your sin.
Call on Him now and He'll take you in.
Have you considered the Saviour today?
> Are you lost and undone? Just kneel down and pray.
> Give your heart to Jesus, He's the only way.
> Have you considered the Saviour today?

His Ring

I used to live safe and sound in my Father's home, but my stubborn heart led me down a lonely road.

~ If Only ~

I took flight with the wealth my Father gave to me.
Like a fool I wasted all, living life so sinfully.
When I had nothing left and all my friends were gone,
I came to realize how all my choices had been wrong.
So I went back to my Father, confessing all my sins.
I said, let me be your servant, but please just take me in.

> But He put a ring upon my finger, shoes upon my feet,
> the finest robe across my back.
> For me, He made a joyous feast.
> Just to be His servant, I would have done anything,
> but with tender love and mercy,
> my Father gave to me His ring.

I know it's not my place to tell you how to live your life,
for I've surely caused my share of misery and strife.
But the pain that's deep within your heart, I can clearly see.
Brother, I once stood there in your shoes.
Here's what the Lord has done for me.

> But He put a ring upon my finger, shoes upon my feet,
> the finest robe across my back.
> For me, He made a joyous feast.
> Just to be His servant, I would have done anything,
> but with tender love and mercy,
> my Father gave to me His ring.

He wrote this song for Tony and Adrianna and sang it at their wedding.

'Til There Was You

Not so long ago, I spent all my time alone,
never knowing there was you.
Every day was bitter cold and kept me chilled down to the bone.
Tell me, what was I to do?
Then the Lord, in all His grace, revealed to me your shining face.

> 'Til there was you, I never saw a sunrise.
> Couldn't see through all the tears that were in my eyes.
> 'Til there was you, every day seemed to be a false start.
> Couldn't breathe for all the pain down in my broken heart.
> But God pulled me through my storm,
> I've never felt so safe and warm.
> Now I take your hand before Him,
> thankful that He helped me make it through 'til there was you.

Life has many ups and downs and many ins and outs.
God gives us bad with all the good.
And though I'd heard all this before,
I didn't know if life would start o'er.
Didn't know if it could.

Repeat chorus
'Til there was you.

Jason

Jason wrote this poem as he pondered whether or not he should ask Renee out for a date.

Your World

I shake the globe and gaze inside.
Quietly the glittering snow falls all around your world,
sparkling from the reflection of your bright smile.
I can only imagine the joy within your heart,
for I am trapped outside the crystal dome.

I raise the blinds to look out my window,
nature's magnificence complimenting
your rare beauty.
My spirit falls, for I am not with you.
I am sealed behind these panes.

I open my scrapbook and travel back through time
to wonderful days gone by.
I see our happy faces and try to relive our precious moments,
but they are locked within the colors of the prints.

Jason wrote "Vapor" the night he finally did ask Renee out for their first date.

Vapor

You stand as close to me as my very breath,
yet to my heart you are an illusion.
How could you be anything more
when I have been nothing more than that to you?

Oh, for strength to reveal my longing.
Oh, for understanding, that I might know your heart
and that you might know mine.
Oh, for that perfect opportunity
to share just an instant of time to see if the candle
    will hold a flame.

Has that moment passed? Have I let it slip away
like water through my fingers? Has it come
in the darkness and burned off
as the morning fog, never to be seen again?

I pray not. I ask the Lord each night for rainfall,
to lower you sweet vapor over me once more.

Jason wrote these poems as he and Renee dated:

My Someday

You ask about the silence and the thoughts in my head.
I look at you and try to speak but sigh again instead.

If only I could make you feel the way I feel inside,
then maybe I could finally stop this roller coaster ride

of highs and lows that I go through each day.
You talk and smile and laugh with me
and then you drive away.

I try to tell myself you're a friend and nothing more,
but these feelings I have are too strong to ignore.

And as I sit and talk with you, I realize the déjà vu.
I know we haven't seen each other for a long while,
but it seems like we've walked together many miles.
You know me more than anyone, and I think that I know you.
I just hope that someday we'll be one instead of two.

Before you speak, there's one last thing I've got to tell.
Now you know from all I've said that I really fell,
but if you say that friends is how we must stay,
then I'll take that, but deep inside, I'll still hope for my someday.

Dreaming

I can see that you are holding back, trying to take things slow, working so hard to keep yourself from letting go.

Your eyes are going back in time, thinking of way back when 'cause you've been hurt before and don't want to go through that again.

Let me put your mind at ease. I know we'll be just fine.
I promise to always be yours, if you promise to be mine.

Lately I've been dreaming of me and you,
and I believe there's nothing we can't do.
We've already been to Paris and seen the Eiffel Tower standing tall. Last night we strolled hand in hand
as the sun set over Niagara Falls.
So see? You don't need to worry like you do.

Do you fear that you should never give your heart away again?
I know you said that life's too short to spend it fighting with a man. It won't be that way this time if you give your heart to me.
Just close your eyes and hold me close,
it can be just like my dreams.

I've seen us holding to each other through good times and the bad. We'll always be sweethearts and friends, even when we're mad.
So see? There's no need to worry like you do.
I've already seen how we will be
when I'm dreaming of me and you.

Jason wrote this after becoming engaged to Renee:

When Good-Bye Becomes Good Night

When "good-bye" becomes "good night"
and the object of my dreams
lives safe within my sight,

loneliness will take its dying breath
before giving up the fight.

When our "someday" becomes "tomorrow"
and our plans are made complete,
I will finally outlive my solitary sorrow,
at last laying down my grief, and from my Lord your
    joy I'll borrow.

When morning come and you are here with me,
my heart will give out peaceful sighs.
Embracing life within your loving arms will be
the delightful task I'll perform each day
until Jesus calls us to eternity.

Jason wrote "Three Rings" as his wedding vows.

Three Rings

With three rings I thee wed
and forever pledge my heart to you.
From this day forward, through every test,
I will prove my love is true.

The first I gave when I asked for your hand.
It is of course the engagement ring.
A token to you, my dearest of friends,
of the joy that makes my soul sing.

Today I place the second, which is the twin to mine.
A symbol of our union, it is the wedding ring,

shining bright for all the world to see,
you are my queen and I your king.

The last I will give as often as you need
through the storms that life shall bring,
that you may trust and on me lean,
for when you suffer, I also will be suffering.